THE
MERCY
JOURNALS

THE
MERCY
JOURNALS

CLAUDIA CASPER

ARSENAL PULP PRESS
VANCOUVER

THE MERCY JOURNALS
Copyright © 2016 by Claudia Casper

ARSENAL PULP PRESS
Suite 202 – 211 East Georgia St.
Vancouver, BC V6A 1Z6
Canada
arsenalpulp.com

The publisher gratefully acknowledges the support of the Canada Council for the Arts and the British Columbia Arts Council for its publishing program, and the Government of Canada (through the Canada Book Fund) and the Government of British Columbia (through the Book Publishing Tax Credit Program) for its publishing activities.

This is a work of fiction. Any resemblance of characters to persons either living or deceased is purely coincidental.

Illustrations by Adam Meuse
Cover and text design by Oliver McPartlin
Edited by Susan Safyan

Printed and bound in Canada

Library and Archives Canada Cataloguing in Publication

Casper, Claudia, 1957-, author

    The Mercy journals / Claudia Casper.

Issued in print and electronic formats.

ISBN 978-1-55152-633-1 (paperback).—ISBN 978-1-55152-634-8 (html)

    I. Title.

PS8555.A778M47 2016   C813'.54   C2015-908284-6

                                                C2015-908285-4

To James Griffin, the love of my life

On October 15, 2072, two Moleskine journals were found wrapped in shredded plastic inside a yellow dry box in a clearing on the east coast of Vancouver Island near Desolation Sound. They were watermarked, mildewed, and ragged but legible, though the script was wildly erratic. Human remains of an adult male were unearthed nearby along with a shovel and a 9mm pistol. Also found with the human remains were those of a cougar. The journals are reproduced in their entirety here, with only minor copy-editing changes for ease of reading.

JOURNAL
ONE

My name is Allen Levy Quincy. Age 58. Born May 6, 1989. Resident of Canton Number 3, formerly Seattle, Administrative Department of Cascadia.

This document, which may replace any will and testament I have made in the past, is the only intentional act of memory I have committed since the year 2029. I do not write because I am ill or because I leave much behind. I own a hot plate, three goldfish, my mobile, my Callebaut light, my Beretta M9, the furniture in this apartment, and a small library of eleven books.

I sit at my kitchenette island in this quasi-medieval, wired-by-ration, post nation-state world, my Beretta on my left, bottle of R & R whiskey on my right, speaking to the transcription program on my mobile.

I was sober for so long. Eighteen years. I was sober through what seems to have been the worst of the die-off. Three and a half to four billion people, dead of starvation, thirst, illness, and war, all because of a change in the weather. The military called it a "threat multiplier."

You break it, you own it—the old shopkeeper's rule. We broke our planet, so now we owned it, but the manual was only half written and way too complicated for anyone to understand. The winds, the floods, the droughts, the fires, the rising oceans, food shortages, new viruses, tanking economies, shrinking resources, wars, genocide—each problem spawned a hundred new ones. We finally managed to get an international agreement with stringent carbon emissions rules and a coordinated plan to implement carbon capture technologies, but right from the beginning the technologies either weren't effective enough or caused new problems, each of which led to a network of others. Within a year, the signatories to the agreement, already under intense economic and political pressure, were disputing who was following the rules, who wasn't, and who had the ultimate authority to determine non-compliance and enforcement.

Despite disagreements, the international body made headway controlling the big things—coal generators, fossil fuel extraction, airplane emissions, reforestation, ocean acidification—but the small things got away from them—plankton, bacteria, viruses, soil nutrients, minute bio-chemical processes in the food chain. Banks and insurance companies failed almost daily, countries went bankrupt, treaties and trade agreements broke down, refugees flooded borders, war and genocide increased. Violent conflict broke out inside borders, yet most military forces refused to kill civilians. Nation-states collapsed almost as fast as species became extinct. Eventually the international agreement on climate change collapsed completely, and the superpowers retreated behind their borders and bunkered down. The situation was way past ten fingers, eleven holes; it was the chaos that ensues after people miss three meals and realize there's no promise of a meal in the future.

Our dominion was over.

A group of leaders—politicians, scientists, economists, religious and ethnic leaders, even artists—people with a vision, called a secret conference with the remaining heads of state and emerged with an emergency global government, agreed-upon emergency laws, and enforcement protocols. The new laws included a global one-child limit and a halt to all CO_2 emissions. The provision of food and health care to as many people as possible was prioritized, along with militarily enforced peace, severe power rations, and further development of renewable energy. The agreement was for one year, but it's been renewed every year for the past fifteen.

Why am I voicing all this? You already know it, I already know it, but I rehearse the events again and again, looking for what we could have done differently; there were so many things, so many ways we could have avoided most of the deaths, but really, were we ever going to act differently? I pour another drink. I drink it.

I was sober through most of that history. I stayed sober when my ex-wife died of a deadly new variant of the hantavirus that had spread north, and I stayed sober when I took care of my sons. Sober even though they acted like I was the volatile element in their lives and looked only at each other when I spoke to them. When I left for work and listened at the door, they finally became animated and relaxed enough to be afraid of everything else in the world crashing down on them. I tried to be tender with them, to lay my hand on their heads, put an arm around their shoulders, but they'd wince or stay perfectly still. I was sober through all that.

But now I'm drunk.

Last week I went out and got a mickey of whiskey from the bootleg. This week, a bottle a night is barely touching it, so I went down to the corner. It was still the corner. I'm not fussy, I told the guy, just get me out of my mind. He hunched deep in his coat, causing his demi-gray ponytail to fan out at the collar. He sucked mucus in and horked, a gesture communicating both his contempt and camaraderie for his customers. Whole ecosystems have vanished but ...

Ambien, O.C.? I suggested. Triple C, anything. Walking away with four pills in my pocket, I passed a scattering of young women and men trying to get shelter in a loading bay from a wind that peppered us all hard with squally rain. They looked like they were waiting for a delivery. I felt sorry for them and hoped it wasn't long in coming.

I don't know what he sold me—something new: Mimosa. You'll feel mellow as butter in ten minutes, he said, with no weirdness. I dropped by the bootleg and bought a couple of bottles just in case. Took a slug, wrapped a sweater round one of the bottles so they wouldn't clank in my pack, and headed for home. I started to feel the relief of knowing I had something that would bring relief. A few blocks from my apartment I got dizzy, which happens periodically since my condition started. I managed to make it to a small park and lean against one of the scrawny trees the city planted to replace the ones that keeled over in the last windstorm. I lay my cheek up against its cool, wet bark and closed my eyes. I don't know how long it took for my head to clear, ten minutes, two hours, but eventually I opened my eyes again. I was staring at the sparse grass at my feet. The earth between some of the blades began to move as pea-sized balls of dirt were pushed up from below. Then I glimpsed what was pushing the dirt—worms—purply-pink, the colour of cold lips.

They finished clearing out the entrances to their holes and popped out, eight of them, sticking up like baby fingers. They were a real demographic mix—from young to old, hermaphroditic to gendered, light pink to medium purple. They waved their stick arms in cheery exuberance and were almost endearing, if you can say that about worms. They smiled at me like they knew me, then glanced at each other in nervous excitement, and one of them counted off, *A one, and a two, and a one, two, three* ... They broke into song, harmonizing like a barbershop octet, with fake British accents:

> *Allen Quincy, Allen Quincy,*
> *Don't be chintzy*
> *Drop your martyr*
> *Join the partyr!*

My mind started to thrash about inside my skull, trying to find any excuse not to accept. It was a nice invitation, and I didn't want to be rude.

I'm working very early in the morning, I said lamely. *I need my sleep.* The worms dropped their heads, crushed with disappointment, and nodded. I was scared. I'd met those worms before, but not for a long time, not for twenty years, not

16

since I was sober. I thought they'd be back; they're persistent little buggers. I wasn't sure I could hold them off this time.

I raced home, too alarmed now to try a pill. I flushed all four down the toilet, got my 9mm out of the closet, loaded it, put the safety on, and careened around my apartment, chilled with sweat, weeping, moaning, pressing against the walls. I sank to the floor on the cracked linoleum of the kitchenette, the Cracked Linoleum Trials of Allen Quincy, and cracked. My heart can live with what's in my mind—the heart is a cold and calculating organ—but my mind can't.

I couldn't bear another minute in my head, let alone the rest of my life. Like a man drowning I wrenched my mobile off its dock on the generator and croaked the words, obliteration, memory. The search engine spewed out useless entries: Hacktivists Breach Secret Service Servers, Buddhas of Bamiyan, Damnatio memoriae, Save Our Libraries, Harry Potter's obliteration charm. I voiced, mind-control, amnesia—the results were equally useless. I cried out, forget and scanned the first ten items: forget-me-nots, Lest We Forget, Forget about Location, Location, Location, etc. I scanned the next fifty. At sixty-one I almost smashed my mobile against the wall and obliterated it. I gargled out the words destruction of memory and there, item thirty-two, after Sands of Destruction GameFaqs, Take Back Our Cultural Memory, Orwell's *1984*, and Alzheimer's, the words popped out: "Writing destroys memory."

I felt in that instant that I had just read my possible salvation.

I clicked on the link and sank onto a kitchen chair.

Psycholinguistics scholar Marjan Rohani of Oxford University, in her work on long-term memory, language, and the hyper-connectivity of the internet, re-examines the implications of the assertion by ancient-Greek philosopher Socrates (as reported by Plato) that the process of writing weakens the mind. "It will implant forgetfulness in [men's] souls; they will cease to exercise memory because they rely on that which is written, calling things to remembrance no longer from within themselves, but by means of external marks." (Phaedrus, Plato)

Oh, for such a weakened mind! I poured a giant whiskey and water, downed it, put the Beretta down on the counter, and voiced the first entry into my mobile. Why wait? I'm not nostalgic.

My name is Allen Levy Quincy. Age 58 ...

I finished the bottle and blacked out.

This morning nothing seems clear. It's as though a clumsy acupuncturist was probing my brain all night trying to activate some kind of release. It hurts, but there's no pain. I text in sick to work—the second time in seventeen years—and stare out the window at a skateboarder on the parking lot roof across the street. His cardigan blows open as he spirals down the interior ramp and pops out into the street, does a quick kick flip off the sidewalk, and disappears.

The world right now—skater heaven. I try to eat a heel of bread, but the smell of the yeast turns my stomach.

How to proceed? This morning it's clear that the words *writing destroys memory* do not mean what they say. How could writing destroy memory? Socrates was indulging in hyperbole. I searched up more about him. He was indignant because the new technology of writing was making students less interested in memorizing poems, speeches, and information and thus weakening their ability to memorize. But memorization is not my problem. The memories that threaten my survival are bolted into the very tissue of my brain. Writing is not going to destroy them.

Patience, Quincy, patience.

There's something there. Something in the writing.

Approach your destroying angels one word at a time.

I'll approach with caution. If I go at my memories directly I'll never survive. I will take the longer road and lay an ambush. I will describe my world. I will tell you about Ruby.

I am creating this document because of her.

Spark to dynamite, grit in oyster, cutter of hair, Eve, Pandora, agitator, gestator of mystery, fomenter of change. Ruby.

There was blood on her teeth when she last walked out the door and gave me a look I am still trying to understand. That was over a week ago, when my old strategy for survival finally imploded.

Eighteen years ago I had also been this desperate. I was on antidepressants, going to group therapy, talk therapy, gaming obsessively online, drinking to blackout—nothing helped enough. The army shrink, a pleasant, amoral, over-worked man, told us that repressing the traumatic memories would not work, but obsessively rehearsing them was also damaging—wearing a groove in our brains, so to speak. One day he told us to write Impact Statements. He said we had to find a way to let ourselves *off the hook*. I walked out the door and never went back. The worms had arrived by then and were popping up randomly to serenade me. Suicide was folding back her sheets and giving me the come hither in an inventive variety of poses.

Then too I'd voiced variations on "forgetting" into the search engine, and the results had been equally useless. Finally I'd tried "remembering," and had landed on an article from the early twenty-first century when governments still funded research not related to immediate survival. The article explained how neuroscientists had discovered that the ability to remember important things depended on the simultaneous ability to block out or forget unimportant details. Since my need was to block memories that were already lodged deep in my brain, I decided to build an anti-mnemonic firewall by jamming my mind full of unimportant details. It took months, it took discipline, it took abandoning my military career for the job of parking-enforcement officer, it took quitting booze, it took the end of my marriage, cutting off friends, and reducing the already uneasy connection with my sons to an even more reserved and distant one. I shrank my life to an existence so small nothing important could penetrate. In the end I don't know if it was the pure, uncontaminated banality of my life, or the controlled, predictable, tiny scope of it that did the trick, but I got relief.

I went to work. Came home. Good citizen. I lived within my rations and fined those who overstepped theirs. Over time, my shrunken life evolved into a kind of monk's existence minus the religion, but you could have also said—it would be ironic but true—that I lived the life of a hedonist. A celibate hedonist. Nothing like my brother's pleasures before the die-off—the yacht, fast cars, waterfront mansion, and five-star vacations. I was a low-end hedonist. I had no dissatisfaction. I wasn't frustrated about anything. I wasn't fixing anything. I was neither building nor destroying. My desires were simple and I was satisfied in satisfying them. Pleasure filled my life.

At night I looked forward to the task of threading my hands and my foot past small tears in the pyjamas I'd had since Jennifer and I split. They'd been laundered to the thickness of gauze. I took pleasure in the feel of my shabby flannel sheets against the skin of my ankles and in the reflected heat from the duck feathers in my duvet. Mornings I watched the eruption of goosebumps on my forearms as my skin re-entered the bracing, damp world. I relished tannin from my tea coating the back of my tongue and watery porridge absorbing the acids in my stomach. I fed my fish and was in awe at these slivers of flashing light in my dun apartment. Even the tiny bubbles that appeared in the sponge when I washed my dishes and the shiny patina of my bowl after I dried it were mesmerizingly beautiful. I liked the way my foot fit into the mould of my boot, and I admired the grey, velvety, thin dawn outside my window. My first step out into the street, always a thrill, marked the daily re-entry into a world animated by jittery, soft shadows and continuous breezes. Even my brain, scarred as it is, gave some pleasure remembering what I'd read the night before or tossing up an image of my sons' slender, hairless arms throwing stones into the sea.

All my cats were stuffed in a bag and sleeping well together. I hardly ever went off the deep end anymore, and when I did I usually had warning. Sometimes I even managed to watch myself calmly in an "out of mind" rather than "out of body" state. In those days, before she walked into my life, I inhabited a barebones state of nirvana, watching the flies buzz hypothermically in the cold air and rivulets of water run into cracks of shattered pavement.

But she showed me for a fake. All my equanimity sprang from one thing, and one thing only, which was not that my life was nearing any kind of enlightenment, not at all. It was that I was dead.

The city was quiet with a quiet that didn't exist before the die-off. No traffic or pile-drivers, leaf blowers or airplanes, just the hum of an occasional electric vehicle, the tinkle of cyclists' bells, and the sound of gears spinning. It was dinnertime, and hardly anyone was about. I was on my way home from work, just passing the community dining hall where people eat to save deductions from their monthly power ration from cooking. The hall's side door by the kitchen was wedged open, and the percussion of plates and cutlery and chairs spilled onto the sidewalk, but instead of the usual roar of conversation, a woman's voice addressed the diners over a sound system. I paused.

You have to OPT out—One Pure Thing—one pure thing to dedicate yourself to, she proclaimed. Freedom or love or nature or community. Opting out gives your life simplicity and purpose. I am opting out for freedom. That's my cause. A trolley full of dirty dishes went by and one of the wheels jammed on a potato peel, so I missed the next part of the speech to the clatter. I started hearing her again at ... never belonged to the corporations, and it doesn't belong to the government either. OneWorld is good enough right now but, she snapped her fingers, like *that* it could change, and what could we do about it? They have all the information, all the records of our civilization in their control, and we have nothing but what we know in our heads and the few books remaining in our libraries and on our bookshelves. That knowledge belongs to us. We made it. Tomorrow we march for the right to elect representatives to protect our birthright! Noon at the old post office!

I've always hated politics. Even before. I get restless at the mere mention. So I simply took it as a sign that things were getting better if people had the energy to demonstrate and continued on my way home. A few blocks later, as I was stepping carefully over a large slab of broken pavement and listening to the wind snap sheets of plastic tacked across the broken windows high up in the old post office, a new sound penetrated my consciousness. *Clack, clack, clack.* It was the kind of sound you don't realize you haven't heard for ages until you hear it, and then you instantly realize how long it's been absent.

The contact of the high heels with the paving was stable and assured, so not a spike heel, I assumed, yet the pitch of the contact was too high and airy for a thick heel. The pace was quick though not clipped or striding. Purposeful.

I am a large man and can defend myself against most members of my species, prosthesis notwithstanding. I am blessed with a dense skeleton and well-defined muscles whose only limitation is lack of flexibility. My hands have the weight of hammers. I don't fear being overpowered by an antagonist but, since my illness, I only have two minutes before I break down. Crying doesn't do it justice. Torrents, gasping, mucusy sobs and tremors. I am trained in Krav Maga and I'm quick, so I haven't failed yet.

The steps came up behind me on the left and a perfume, a complex scent—tea, cloves, freshly mown grass—expanded its radius around me. I knew exactly where she was without looking.

When she passed I could have turned my left hand sideways and grazed her hip with my thumb. I had an impulse to reach for her wrist. My eyes slid to the left and saw her naked foot in a red high-heeled sandal, the skin of her heel callused and slightly cracked, her baby toe turned out. The grey-blue light of the cold January dusk made her skin almost fluorescent. The tendons and muscles of her foot seemed hyper-defined and taut in their attachments to the small bones. Her foot so enchanted me that I only thought to look at her face after she had passed. The back of a large army-green bomber jacket with black trim and gold-buttoned epaulets, possibly from some kind of uniform, flapped open above a brown dress with a fringe of rags. She marched to the end of the block, dark ponytail swinging, turned right, and looked directly at me before disappearing down the street.

I hurried to the corner, hump and stump, hump and stump, but the street was empty. I turned my mobile on to see the time: five-thirty p.m.

I climbed the three floors to my apartment by memory because the only light inside the stairwell is from a skylight. I fumbled my key into the lock, turned it, and opened the door. The living room was dimly visible in the blue glow of other people's lights spilling in from the building's courtyard. My furniture: a green velvet easy-chair, beat-up even by today's existential standards, stuffing bubbling out at the arm and seat cushion; a worn leather ottoman;

a white bookshelf that's wobbly because the hardware's reamed out the disintegrating particleboard; a wooden bar stool; a table with three chairs; my charging station; and flashes of gold under the cool light of my aquarium. I took my coat off and hung it on a hook by the door. That hook, a classic bronze one like we used to have in school locker rooms, is the only change I've made to this apartment.

Billions die from starvation, thirst, disease, and war, violence is done to the mind, a human life shrinks to the emotional range of a hummingbird guarding his territory, cataclysms come and go, yet someone of the opposite sex walks by and really looks at you and your whole world comes to a stop.

I swear that with that first look from the end of the block she saw me—the soul I was born with, the man I had become, and the thorny crosshatch of my life—wounds received and wounds delivered. She saw my strength and my—I won't say weakness—my ruinedness. In that instant, when she looked back, I *knew* she was interested in me. I mean, why not? With my fake leg, the scar on the left side of my face, a body on the downhill slide past fifty, sterling-grey highlights in my hair, and riveting, half-dead eyes, I'd be hard for any woman to pass up, let alone a woman with bare legs striding through the evening haze in red heels.

I went into the kitchen and opened the coolbox. I pride myself on keeping it neat and stocked only with the essentials, yet sometimes I still can't seem to find anything inside it. I could hear my mom—Close the fridge, you're letting the cold out—not that it matters anymore, at least not in winter, because the temperature inside the coolbox is virtually the same as inside our homes.

I stared at a carton of eggs, a packet of sausages, half a bottle of goat milk, and a bowl of puckering apples, unable to remember what I wanted. The sound of heels on the sidewalk echoed in my head, accompanied by the image of pale, slightly blue feet.

I went looking for her the next evening, same route, same routine, hoping she'd repeat her path. I leaned against the wall at the exact point where she'd passed the night before. I looked up at the sky. For once it wasn't raining or windy. Twenty minutes passed. A man walking on the other side of the road stopped and yelled, Hey Mercy! Is that you? What the fuck!

I don't swear. My father stopped swearing near the age of forty-nine when he was doing graduate studies in history for a promotion to Brigadier General and he had what he called an epiphany: swearing devalued the profession. Predictably, he decided to impose his epiphany on his family. My mom, a high-school English teacher, ignored him and kept swearing like a trooper. My younger brother Leo argued that since Dad had had thirty good years of swearing, he and I still had thirty coming before our bill was due.

Leo and I swore, Dad docked our allowance and went around looking disappointed. Leo never did stop. In fact, he swore extra around our father until the day our father died. After I graduated from the Royal Military College in Kingston I got posted immediately to Afghanistan. Over there I noticed the difference between our troops and the Afghani people. We were vulgar and crude, almost pornographic, while they were polite and gracious. I realized my father had been right and stopped swearing.

My buddies found it insufferable. They thought I was acting superior. A fellow officer went after me one night on leave. He was drunk and one of his buddies had recently been killed by an IED, so because it was the booze more than rage I was able to let him punch himself out on me. He threw one last wild blow, fell back on the banquette, lifted his beer off the table, and slowly let it sink back down as he blacked out.

At first it was hard to articulate myself without swearing. It took me forever to find the right words, and I sounded prissy even to myself.

I looked up. Mercy was my army nickname. I called back, Lola? Is that you? What are you doing down here?

He crossed the street. His head was shaved but he had a five o'clock shadow. He was still solid, almost as broad across the shoulders as he was tall, though he looked like he needed a good chiropractor—one of his shoulders was low, and his trunk was torqued to the right. He was wearing his old combat coat.

Yeah man, it's me. Visiting my kid. How the fuck are you?

I have my days. You?

He looked twenty years older, which was about right since it had to be twenty years since I last saw him. Now that we were face to face we were having a bit of trouble with the proximity. He looked at the wall over my shoulder and I looked at the curb to his left.

Never better. Never better. Yeah. Not bad for a fucking old guy.

I switched to looking at the curb to his right.

You seen Mixed Nuts? he asked. I shook my head.

29

Still dumb as shit no doubt. Fuckin' hell. I'm doing the work a machine should be doing—digging, hoeing, loading. At my age. No one knows how to do anything anymore. My back's fucked. They're going to put me on record keeping. Old lady fucked off.

Yeah, well. Join that club.

Saw Randy about a year ago.

Of all the guys I knew, only one of them was still married. Randy. I mean, what are the odds with a name like that? But he was the real deal. Get the job done, move on. Never hopped up, never in a rage, no overkill, just did his job and let it go. We didn't make the world the way it is, he used to say. No second thoughts. He was just as happy pushing a pen as throwing grenades. He tried to mother-hen us all at first, keep us in touch with each other, help us out, but I guess he got tired.

Some of the guys still hang out, from Kandahar, but none from that last group in Mexico. We're not like the vets from the old days. We don't march in parades or drink together at the Legion.

He still doing okay? I asked.

He looked fine. I was in a hurry you know, so we didn't hang. Lola tried to look me in the eyes. I appreciated the effort. He managed for the count of two then looked up the street.

Gotta run. Let's have a beer, eh? Next time.

He pulled me in for a hug and we gave each other backslaps.

Yeah, absolutely. Good seeing you. Take care.

Sure. You too.

The only hurry Lola was in was to get away from me. But that's all right. We understand each other. We're all like that. It's not a problem. We're like a family who has buried a murdered child.

Seeing Lola might have set me off, but I was lucky that day because I was so focused on finding the woman from the day before. I watched him hurry down the road and went back to my wall, looking up at the clouds. I saw her this time before I heard her, or rather, the second I set eyes on her I heard the distant clack-clacking.

She seemed taller from a distance, but it must have been the way she held herself because as the distance between us shrank, she seemed shorter. The scent of freshly turned mossy earth preceded her.

I pulled away from the wall and held my hand out.

Hello, I'm Allen Quincy.

Hello. Ruby. Just Ruby.

Since Jennifer died I've heard plenty of women's voices, but this woman's voice—warm, with the grainy hint of a growl of laughter at the beginning of each utterance—made me feel like I hadn't heard one in years.

I fell in beside her but had to work to keep up because of my peg leg. I was looking at her face: crow's feet on the outside corner of her eye, a brown eye with a shot of green; the redness of her lips, not particularly plump but not thin either, with perfect peaks where the trough under the nose makes a wave; her cheek the colour of milky tea—all of it imprinted on me right away. I wasn't looking where I was going and stepped onto a huge shelf of broken pavement that tilted upward.

I fell back against the building to my right, face up to the sky, and slid to the ground. Although I was sitting I felt as though I was swimming through the city, but with no idea what was up or down. My endocrine system fired up, adrenalin poured from a gland near my recovered liver, my chest tightened, the hairs on the back of my neck stood up like mowed hay, and my testicles moved up and down like a pair of marmots.

Since the die-off large shelves of concrete have broken from flooding and from fallen trees, and the sidewalks often look like a madman took a jackhammer to them. Normally I keep my eyes glued to the ground because if I step unknowingly on pavement that tilts, even as little as twenty degrees, I can be catapulted into a state of extreme vertigo. Then I have to crawl home dragging my prosthetic leg behind me and pressing my shoulder against the façades of buildings for orientation. At intersections I pray that a vehicle doesn't hit me. If a passerby offers help, I ask only that they accompany me across the street without touching me because physical contact can trigger extreme nausea, which makes further movement impossible. The whole scene is hard on the dignity and on my knee. Usually by morning, after a hard-fought night's sleep, the vertigo will have receded.

You don't ever want to meet a woman for the first time in a state like that. She must have continued a few steps, then turned around and come back. She crouched in front of me and I could feel the heat coming at me from her open jacket. I prayed she wouldn't touch me.

I'll be fine in a while, I said. Please, for my sake, go where you were going. I'll see you tomorrow. Same place.

Other people came over and two men started to help me up, lifting me under the arms. Let me lean against the wall, I ordered. It will pass. It just takes time. I turned away from them, spread my arms out, and gripped the cement of the wall with my fingertips. I pressed my cheek against its cold stable surface, willing my nausea to pass, willing the world to stay still. My hands tingled. My chest felt too full. I focused on breathing, not deeply, but regularly, regular in, regular out. I waved them away but no one wanted to leave me alone.

In the end I had to let them take me home. Two men put their necks under my arms and carried me, my head flopping left and right because I couldn't keep track of which way was up. I told them where my key was, and they got me in bed and insisted on programming their numbers into my mobile. I asked them to get me a damp towel and a glass of water before they left.

I heard the door to my apartment close. I lay the back of my hand across the bridge of my nose, breathed out, paused, then slowly let the air return. I opened and closed my hands to relieve the tingling. The nausea eased. Then I heard breathing.

Who's here? I called out, but I thought I knew. Someone came into the bedroom. I tried to open my eyes but everything was still spinning and lurching. I glimpsed Ruby's hair, then had to shut my eyes again.

Have we met before? she asked.

No, I don't believe we have.

Who are you?

As you see. A dizzy one-legged man.

Why were you waiting for me?

I saw you the other day.

Hmm.

My nineteen years of celibacy had been effortless and so complete that not even a kiss had brushed my lips.

What do we do now, Allen Quincy?

It would help if I could open my eyes without the room hurling itself into every dimension known to man. Could we start over tomorrow?

I felt her looking at me. I had never thought of eyes as weapons, or as shields, but I was defenseless, unable to open my eyes and look back at her. I did manage to lift the corner of an eyelid and see her tongue lick her lips and disappear back into her mouth. I had to shut the eyelid again because the ceiling tilted to the floor, the nearby wall whipped past the ceiling, and the light fixture ricocheted off everything. I gripped the side of the mattress.

Her hand covered mine, the inside of her wrist touched the hairy back of my wrist, and she leaned over and pressed her warm lips on my cold ones. It wasn't a kiss so much as an experimental applying of pressure. Her tongue pried where my lips met. I sank fast. I opened my mouth and fell down a whirlpool to the centre of the earth.

I won't write another word. This memory I intend to keep.

The words above, what I've written until now, I have just finished transcribing by pencil onto paper from my mobile. My hand is aching and cramped. I haven't held a writing tool for so long the activity feels only distantly familiar, like snapping Lego pieces together.

·When I began this document the only action for "writing" I could imagine was voicing words into my mobile. My words were transcribed on screen and I saved each entry to a cloudfile named Allen's Oblivion. But two days ago I came home from work and sat and stared at my mobile. My mind writhed with memories and thoughts but my lips were sealed shut.

I fed the goldfish and watched for a while, following the flounce of their long, feathery, pale tangerine fins as they moved.

I poured myself a drink. I needed a brain cushion. I saw my Beretta in the cupboard beside the bottle and had the thought *Get the bullets*, and that triggered the thought, *Is this going to be a suicide entry?* I missed my old strategy—I missed it intensely, the shrunken life, the banal pleasures of the everyday, the routine, oh the routine, but Ruby's presence in my life has slammed that door good and tight.

I sat for hours mutely watching my fish, suppressing the bullet-finding urge, and wracking my brain—*Why can't I write? Writing, what is writing?* A man voices memories alone in a room. Without a witness the act has no reality. The man could be doing anything. *Writing needs a reader.* I had to find a way to publish the entries. But where, where could a person publish words these days? I don't know what the situation will be in the future, but at present bandwidth usage is severely limited and individual access is staggered. News is text only, films are watched at cinemas. Everyone's mobile number has a cloud storage quotient that cannot be exceeded.

Every pie quadrant of OneWorld has a Citizen's News site, but my entries weren't news. A site called "Global Graffiti" was recently launched, a kind of trial balloon established by OneWorld where people can post messages of up to 500 words for twenty-four hours on language walls, comments activated.

I poured another depth charge and went to my armchair. I wanted a minimum number of readers so I posted my voicings under the obscure title "Mnemectomy," and drank until I passed out.

When I got home after work the next day, my graffiti had attracted comments. They were mostly the usual money scams, urgent pleas for funds, offers of sexual services or testosterone boosters, but one was from a fellow vet.

Me too brother. Can't shake the memories. Let me know how the writing thing works out for you. It does seem like a long shot I gotta be honest but if it's any good I'd like to try it myself. Don't know how much longer I can hang on. Your talking worms really sketched me out.

I used to be an altruist, but not any more. When I read that comment, I wanted to smash my mobile screen. I deleted the post immediately. I'm not looking for a conversation. I don't want anyone else inside my head. No readers! No audience!

I pressed my forehead against the coolbox and wept because nothing had changed. My lips still did not move, and my voice remained silent. Memories pounded against the inside of my skull, increasing in violence, claustrophobic, maniacal, explosive. Against such potent antagonists, my strategy seemed silly, far-fetched, a thin, improbable thread to hang survival on. Desperate as a fish out of water, suffocating, frantically needing a solution, I had the thought—*reread your original salvation.* I used more rations, searched through my download of Marjan Rohani's article, and found a glimmer of hope in the lines immediately following what I'd read before: "Plato describes Socrates as claiming that writing is inhuman in that it places outside the mind what can only in reality be in the mind. It turns living thoughts into something inanimate. It reifies, and turns inner processes into manufactured things."

Could that be the flaw in my process? Did the act of writing have to produce a physical object, a piece of paper, a book, something that, if I died, would continue beyond me? Voicing only created digitized codes reliant both on a continuous flow of electricity and an information storage system.

Paper and pen. They haven't been around since the late '30s. Trees are no longer cut down, recycled cellulose became too degraded to use, and all farmed plant matter is used for food. With no paper there's been no need to produce writing implements. I hurried to my bedroom and pulled out the suitcase where I keep a few mementos. Inside were two journals and a box of twenty pencils.

After my mother died, when my brother Leo and I were searching for her will, we found two old blank journals in the bottom drawer of her desk with a box of fresh pencils. We never found a will and because my mother died just as the die-off was peaking, Leo and I agreed to leave her possessions as they were for the time being and each just take one thing. I was in bad shape then, as bad as now, so I just took the first thing I thought of—the journals and the pencils. Leo annoyed me by taking a long time to choose, rifling through everything before eventually settling on our father's hunting knife.

The journals are black, soft-covered, bound with two staples. The first page of one of them had a paragraph of writing, my mother's writing:

Today I am seventy-eight. I have been blessed with a good life but I am afraid for the future, for my sons and for my grandchildren. Perhaps nothing really matters in the end, but I desperately want them to survive. If they die too then truly nothing will be left of me. I was born January 31, 1955, ten years after the end of World War II, and it looks like I will die before World War III ends, if that's what people are going to call this. I'm alone. My husband

died two years ago and my sons and daughters-in-law do
their duty but not more. None of us have the energy.

I read with the warm rasp of my mother's voice reso-
nating through me, and the abrupt absence of any further
words was deafening. I grinned, but it was not a grin accompanied by any feeling of pleasure. Rather it was the kind of
grin that's meant to ward off a threat or recognize a threat
disguised as something else.

I tore out the page, folded it, and tucked it in the back.

Her journal will be the container, the object, external to
me in which I enter what is anguished and exterminating.
By giving the memories that threaten me existence outside
myself, I hope to degrade their presence inside me and pry
loose their death grip on my mind. Once I finish writing this
document and close the cover of this journal, my story will
be sealed inside, until perhaps an unknown reader in the
future, with cool detachment, opens its faded black cover
and reads: *My name is Allen Levy Quincy. Age 58. Born May 6,
1989.*

That is the only reader I can write for.

You might be thinking that Ruby was a bit on the easy side, promiscuous even. Definitely not fussy. Such thoughts crossed my mind too, especially the not fussy part, but as far as desire for her was concerned, those thoughts crossed the room and just kept right on going out the door.

She was a force field.

Having sex with her was like colliding with a meteorite.

The closest comparison I can make is to a fight where afterward, the only thing left is a whirlwind of impressions of violence: bone underneath flesh, something striking your jaw, the feeling of striving against gravity and, at the end, you stand up and you're still alive and time winks and goes back to normal. You know you're probably hurt, but you can't feel it yet; you're not sure how badly your opponent is hurt or even if the fight is really over.

I surfaced the next morning, red lipstick on my face and tangled sheets the only proof I had that I hadn't dreamt the whole thing. A flurry of images and sensations came at me— red mouth, green rods in her brown eyes, long dark hair against my cadaver skin, an open mouth laughing, startling in its lack of missing teeth, breasts dense, small, and close to the chest, muscular haunch, and in the middle, myself, dizzy but closing in at every turn, the synesthesia caused by my vertigo making everything smell of the sea and fresh dirt.

It was six a.m. when I stepped out the door, exultant and clear-headed. The streets were empty, the fog thick. When there's no wind, the fog usually hangs around all day except for maybe a couple of hours in the afternoon when it lifts to mere cloud. On the rare occasions when the sun comes out, people rush to wash their clothes and hang them out to dry. In spring, farmers check their watches and count the hours to see when they need to roll the tarps back over seedlings and less hardy crops so they don't burn. Birds and insects take cover. Nature becomes still until the cloud cover rolls back in.

I walked down the street, stump and foot, stump and foot, throwing my peg leg out in front of me like a land paddle, cooked oats and tea warming the inside of my ribs. Over the years I've come to like the new rhythm of my gait, the syncopated double beat, the rubber thud of my real foot followed on the off-beat by the higher-pitched shuffle-pad of the prosthesis in its shoe. I picked a simple prosthesis, a single-axis, constant-friction model with an adjustable cell that prevents the shank from swinging forward too fast. I've never regretted it.

I felt exultant, yes, light-footed and bouncy, yes, but also like a man who had been picked out of a herd and savaged. Far behind my happiness, in the dark shadows at the farthest back of backstage, was a whisper of alarm. I ignored the whisper and focused on how the morning light changed gradually from dark slate to pearl, and the sky's weight changed from a blanket of darkness to a basement ceiling of wet stone to swirling white mist. The dark green leaves of vines on buildings threw no shadows in the grey light.

I walked through the old Chinatown below the viaduct where the majority of buildings are abandoned. The ones that are inhabited are packed with people. Pink or yellow insulation cannibalized from empty houses has been tacked up inside windows and doors and stapled to ceilings to keep in the warmth. The neighbourhood looks like a gang of twelve-year-olds swept through and turned everything into a backyard fort. I made my way along the broken sidewalk that I have to take now that the viaduct has been condemned. I miss walking high above the city, mountains and ocean to the left, sky surrounding my head.

Still, on the route under the viaduct I get to see street art, which is miraculously appearing again. I passed a painting I particularly like of a giant, bald, putty-coloured man peeping over a stone wall. One of his eyes, which are emerald green, had broken off, exposing the rusty rebar beneath. I found the missing chunk and leaned it against the wall, so one eye looked up at the other.

As usual, I arrived at the Civic Security Station at 6:45 a.m. Velma looked up from the desk, bundled in two sweaters and a scarf, her dyed red hair done up stiff as a pine tree, her skin white and pouchy and covered in a flesh-toned powder that made the tiny hairs on her face unmistakable. She frowned. The changes in the world have left her irritable, and she probably won't cheer up before she dies. She wants to blame somebody for encouraging her to believe that the old world was real in some absolute, permanent way. She'd been pacing herself for life in that reality and says she has no interest in making adjustments to this new one. She feels ripped off, like someone should pay, but has no idea who so she's always on the lookout.

I myself was done with the old world.

Done.

My old house had abutted the freeway, which was how Jennifer and I could afford to buy off the base. We could taste the exhaust. Every night sixteen lanes of drivers sat in their cars, waiting to get where they were going. Taillights and headlights, strings of them, extending out of sight—drivers impatient to get out of the city, drivers impatient to get in. Everyone knew, on some level, that it couldn't go on. The sheer numbers of us precluded it. I was planning to move my family up to Mom's cabin. I'd laid in a rifle, ammunition, seeds, canned food, water purification kits, loads of matches, a generator. The key would be knowing when to leave the city for good. The Green Planet Brigade started to bomb roads. In retrospect, I see that would have been the time to leave, but you never leave with the first big crisis, because you think it might be a one-off and there's all the other noise on the bandwidth—the promise of quantum computing, of physicists harnessing the energy of the geospace vacuum, nuclear fission plants, etc., etc. Then the next crisis hits, and you're already invested in riding it out. You've already adapted to the new pattern. Anyway, Jennifer and I were glad the Green Planet Brigade was doing what they were doing. We thought it might be the beginning of something good.

When I *was* certain it was time to leave, I was on a bus headed south to the Mexican border, and Jennifer and the boys had moved back to the base. She had no way to reach the cabin by herself.

A whisper of warning. *No thinking about the past.* I smacked myself in the head in the change room. Put my uniform on. Ruby's presence had already, after only one night together, made a chink in my armour.

Velma snapped her fingers in front of my face. Hey. Pretty boy. Here's your scanner.

Larry, who works in vehicle reclamation, came out of the can wearing his bright yellow jacket with reflector tape and our unit name, Transpo—Squad B. He looks like the bloodhound version of a human being—baggy flesh, enormous eyes, grey face. He doesn't look well. Maybe heart disease, maybe cancer—the blood isn't moving where it should, but you'd think he didn't have a care in the world.

Quincy. You're looking kind of cheery. What happened, you get laid? Zipping up his fly.

I couldn't help grinning ear to ear.

No way. Really?

Just pulling one of your three legs, you over-privileged bastard, I said.

Always with the gimp card.

At least he's got a card to play, Velma said.

Well, Sunshine, Larry clapped his hands, we men have got work to do.

Nail 'em to the wall, boys.

Don't you love it when she calls us boys? I opened the door.

Our shift starts early so we can catch overnighters and charge them double. It's like hunting, but it's only mice we're after. My job is to walk past every vehicle parked within my territory once an hour and scan the licence plates. The scanner relays data to city hall, which tracks each plate hourly and bills the user. These days the hourly fee for parking is equal to the average person's hourly wage. If a citizen fails to pay parking fees, the vehicle is ticketed and impounded, and their driving privileges are revoked for a month. After four infractions, the penalty is loss of driving privileges for three years.

My job also includes ensuring the vehicles parked in my territory adhere to the latest regulations. When OneWorld came into being, most vehicles were Phevs, Bevs, or hybrids that used various combinations of hydrogen, solar, and electric batteries or fuel cells, with some gasoline or bio-diesel fuel, although some drivers still had luxury models with powerful engines run solely on fossil fuels. These models were banned immediately, but people got fuel on the black market and continued to drive them, either to circumvent charges to their ration cards or to avoid the limits to the speed or distance they could drive. A big part of parking enforcement in those days involved tagging and impounding these vehicles and disenfranchising the transgressors. That particular excitement has diminished over the years since most of the illegal vehicles have been impounded and OneWorld is transitioning to government-owned Shuvs. We still catch the occasional transgressor, though, someone who has installed an illegal engine in an approved body or attached a counterfeit licence plate to an illegal model.

I like to keep my territory clean and orderly. I enjoy catching cheaters. I think of them as people who would steal food from a baby, people who would take my last breath of air without blinking.

Between eight and nine a.m., the streets are full of people going to work, running errands, taking their kids to school. No one is in a hurry, and the city unfolds the way I imagine a medieval town would have—people greeting each other, picking up food, flirting, yawning, waking up as they go—colours faded, buildings ramshackle. Vehicle traffic is less with each passing year. Fewer people, more bicycles. The Canton laid off twenty percent of us in the last two years. I'm lucky to still have my job.

I was making a final round before lunch when an unusual matte sheen on a vehicle caught my eye. I took my key out, got down on my good knee, stuck my prosthesis out to the side, and scratched the solar paint under the bumper. Sure enough, old paint showed through—robin's egg blue. I went and rubbed the tailpipe with my thumb. The soot smelled acrid and metallic. I popped the hood. I don't know how the guy that drove this thing got here without being swarmed because that engine would have sounded louder than any other vehicle around today. I quickly closed the hood and examined the edges of the licence plate. Counterfeit.

I went to the stash box at the end of the block, unlocked it, got out a boot, came back, and clamped it on. Scanned the plate. The parking was paid. I sent in a tow request and moved down the street. I was about four or five cars down the road when I heard the boot being shaken and someone yell, What the fuck!

I scanned the next plate without turning around.

Hey! You! Did you put the boot on me?

I didn't respond.

You. Asshole. Did you boot me? Am I a ghost? Did I fucking up and die and no one told me? This piece of shit life.

The voice was getting closer.

It struck me as familiar in a déjà vu kind of way. I turned and faced him. In these kinds of situations, the Krav Maga comes in handy. When I turned, he stopped. The guy was covered in hair—beard down to his armpits, greying hair down to his elbows. He had a dirty face, blue eyes burning at me. His clothes were dark and dusty, maybe black, maybe charcoal grey, maybe brown, but his shoes were polished and expensive. He must've kept some good pairs from the old days, and he'd recently oiled the leather.

You're driving an illegal model, sir. And you might want to keep your voice down. The public doesn't take kindly to these types of infractions.

Though the crises seem to be on the wane, people are still volatile. No doubt everything will be different in the future and, in any case, I don't want to paint a picture of humanity gone to the dark side—it wasn't like those old Hollywood movies about the future where everyone starts turning into killers and eating each other—mostly people help each other, pool their efforts, try to survive together, but there have been incidents where mobs suddenly coalesce and kill someone who they think is breaking the new environmental laws.

I don't agree with it. Obviously I believe that civil society is our only hope, yet I understand what drives the rage. People still remember when individual citizens were allowed to consume as much as they wanted as long as they could pay. People still remember the impotence of knowing that the environment we all depended on for survival was being destroyed by people wanting more—more money, more security, more control, more stuff—and we remember our own anxiety as we ourselves did things that contributed to our destruction. We remember when we realized that we relied for survival on a system that was killing us. It's not like our fates aren't all bound together. And everyone lost someone close in the die-off. So now, when someone breaks the new laws, people aren't always reasonable.

The bearded guy took a long bead on me.

What is this life to me? he said. Surviving to survive? I don't give a flying fuck about what the public thinks, now do I?

Larry pulled up, which meant that certain things were out of my hands. He unrolled his window and pointed his thumb at the infractor.

Is he giving you a hard time?

Reclaimers like Larry are armed. A couple of passersby stopped and watched the three of us.

I looked at the infractor, and he looked right back at me. Was he just an aggressive prick or was there something else? People were starting to gather to see what the commotion was. I thought he understood that his life was in my hands. He didn't flinch, yet neither did he take the next step.

We were just discussing, Larry, what we'd like to do to people who cheat the system. We're incensed. We're just incensed.

Yeah, well, how do you think we got here in the first place? A lot of assholes in our species, let's face it, Larry said as he leaned out of the driver's side window. Comes with the territory, he said. Natural selection never got rid of 'em, so we have to. He pulled ahead and backed the truck up at an angle to the booted vehicle.

Everybody references evolution these days. I guess coming face to face with extinction does that. If the last half a century showed us anything, it's that human behaviour is not as malleable as we might have thought. It's like our species is on a boat so enormous that no matter how hard we turn the wheel, it takes centuries to register a change in direction, and meanwhile everything around the ship changes a million times over.

Larry got out and took the boot off, lay down on the road, and looked under the vehicle. More people gathered.

Larry, my friend, I said by way of a hint that we might be finding ourselves in a situation, I want to get back to the office for lunch.

He came out from under, sized up the gathering group, and grinned. Yeah, Allen, now that you mention it, I'm bloody hungry too. Why don't you two hop in, and I'll give you a ride?

A young guy, shaved head, medium height, built, called out from the crowd, Who's he, then? and jerked his head toward the infractor who still faced me. And why's he—he jerked his head toward Larry—looking under that vehicle?

The questioner had me stumped. Usually infractors are aware of the danger they're in and slink away as fast as possible. I'd never been in this position before, and I had no idea what to answer—A friend? A passerby? A beggar? I didn't think the crowd would buy any of those.

Him? Larry answered for me. Just some nutcase who wants to change the world. Larry opened the driver's side door, lowered the hook, got out his jack, and went around to the front of the offending vehicle. Hop in, boys, he said to us, but the young guy moved between us and the truck and the crowd followed. The questioner looked at the infractor's feet.

Those are some fancy shoes, he said in a hyper-loud voice, playing to the crowd. How's he want to change the world then? He asked me the question.

The infractor had been looking at me the whole time. I figured he was crazy, but when you looked at him, looked him in the eye, he didn't seem crazy.

You can go, the young man said to me, nodding at my uniform.

It would start as a beating. There was no predicting how far it would go. Climate vigilantism was not prosecuted yet. The government wasn't strong enough, and the rage was too strong. Someone in the crowd yelled out, Cheaters are killers! and in response another voice called out, Absolute adherence!

You're wrong, I started to say. This man is not the driver of that car. He's ... Here I tripped up. I had no plausible explanation for him.

Who the hell are *you*? the infractor yelled at the young man. His voice was louder than the young man's by a factor of ten. Everyone went quiet.

One of the new fascists? You posturing skinhead scum! Who the hell ... The questioner launched himself at the infractor and punched him in the jaw with a force that sent his head cracking back, then rammed him to the ground with his shoulder. The questioner took a step back, then kicked him in the stomach. The infractor groaned. The crowd moved in. I don't know why I got involved because the infractor seemed not to care what happened to himself. Maybe it was because I was standing so close or because Ruby had just opened me up like an oyster shucker, but I went in and punched the questioner in the head. I got him in a plumb, my forearms on either side of his neck, hands clasped behind his head, and kneed him a couple of times in the liver. I whispered, Get lost now or I'm going to kill you. He nodded.

Several people in the crowd had begun to kick the infractor, but I landed a few more blows and pulled him back to his feet. The crowd backed off, but no more than a couple of feet.

I stood beside him and shouted to them, You're wrong— you're dead wrong about him. Larry heard me and started to drive gingerly into the crowd. I locked elbows with the infractor and held my arm out to push the crowd back.

We reached the truck, and Larry popped the passenger door. I pushed the infractor in ahead of me, but had difficulty climbing up with my leg. By the time Larry ordered the infractor to lean out and give me a hand, the questioner had come back with something to prove. He threw a punch at the back of my head. My endocrine went into hyper-drive. I unleashed on him, this time making sure he wasn't getting back up. I tried not to kill him but I know I broke bones and teeth. When I turned back to the truck door, Larry reached past the infractor and yanked me in. I started to tremble top to bottom and stared out the side window as we drove away. Tears ran down my cheeks, yet even then, in that stressed state, I sensed something about the guy in the middle seat. There was something about him. The bulk of him next to me felt different from other people.

Larry took us to the impound lot. I stayed in the truck, working to bring myself back in. He brought us two cups of hot sweet tea. My mom always told me to drink something, any liquid, to stop tears when I was a kid.

I had a scratch on my check, a sore scalp, and sore ribs. The infractor had a bloody nose, a swollen eye, scraped hands, and probably bruised or broken ribs. We got out of the truck. Larry unloaded the vehicle and returned to us.

You can say goodbye to ever driving again. He demanded the infractor's identity card, keyed in the particulars. The infractor watched closely.

You want a drive to the office? Larry asked me.

Sure. Yeah.

And how about you? Larry looked at the infractor.

He nodded.

I cleaned up in the office washroom and let Velma confirm my companion's information and tell him what to expect by way of penalty. He was still hanging around the front door when I came out. He'd wiped his bloody nose on his sleeve.

Sorry for giving you a hard time, he said.

Yeah, well. Times are hard.

I have nowhere to go.

No home?

The wife kicked me out. I gave her everything and then, "my behaviour was maladaptive." Just as everything was going to shit.

That's a long time ago, man. You're milking it a bit, aren't you?

I can't get hooked up.

Why not?

I'm an outlaw.

I shrugged and turned to go for lunch. I was hungry.

You don't know me, do you?

I stopped and turned back. Something about you seems familiar. There's something about your voice.

I'm your brother, asshole.

I looked into the burning eyes I'd been avoiding. How could I not have seen it? True, I wasn't looking for connection with the outside world, even less with a cheater, but I should have known him, even after twenty years, even with the hair and the beard.

I suppose that means I have to keep you? I said.

I let Leo have my shower that night. Then I fed him. Then I'd had enough of him. He complained that there was no booze in the place. I wrapped a sheet around a pile of my clothes for a mattress, gave him the seat cushion from the easy chair for a pillow and my army blanket to supplement his coat and retreated to my bedroom.

I wanted to be rid of him. It was Ruby I wanted to find and bring back to my apartment, not my brother. I had worked seventeen years with pure discipline to tamp down my past, and now here was this hairy, smelly, demanding emanation threatening my hard-won equilibrium because he had nowhere else to go?

But as I folded my clothes and put them away, threaded my way into my pyjamas, turned out the light, and lay on my back waiting for warmth, I remembered how I used to crawl into Leo's bed after a nightmare even though I was the older brother, and he'd pat my head with his smaller hand and we'd look out the window at the chestnut tree as I whispered my nightmare to him, and he'd say, Don't worry. Hamschen (our dead pet hamster) is watching over us, and we'd start to giggle and drift back to sleep together. I remembered that he always used to ask me to feel his muscles, and they were just tendon and bone, like a frog's quad grafted onto a humerus, and he'd be looking at me with unguarded hope. When my own boys were that age and they did the same thing, I'd feel their walnut-sized biceps, knowing they wanted serious acknowledgement, but all I had was affection and the memory of Leo underneath.

Sometime in the middle of that night, with Leo sleeping in the living room, I sat up and was flooded by memories of my old life. I missed Jennifer so much. I think I'd been reliving in my sleep the last time we'd had sex, and I kept trying to wind the dream back the way you used to rewind a DVD by jumping back a chunk, watching a bit of the beginning of the previous scene, then jumping back to the beginning of the chunk before. I was making love with her, and then the dream would leap back to making love when the kids were little, then to when Jennifer was pregnant, then to before we had kids when I returned from a tour in Afghanistan and the sexual excitement was explosive, so to speak, but the dream kept sliding back to the last time we'd made love and somehow Ruby was there but invisible.

I'd come home from Mexico, before the final collapse of the United States of North America, my last tour of duty, and we only managed to get back because we'd carried all the fuel for the return journey with us on the buses when we deployed. I was going through the motions of being a father to the boys—picking them up, swinging them round—but I was numb inside. Everyone in the military knew about PTSD by then, but somehow I figured my life had to have been threatened for me to have it. Jennifer and I made love that first night I came back, and I managed to hide what was going on inside my head, but after that I always begged off tired.

A year later, I took her out for a romantic dinner at one of the few restaurants still running in all the chaos and talked obsessively about the Mexican landscape, the cacti, the rodents and birds and insects. It was her birthday. She asked if I was all right, and I said I was. We drove home through a windstorm, paid the sitter, went upstairs. I kissed her, felt nothing, led her to bed and undressed her, felt nothing, which was, ironically enough, agony. I managed a fragile erection—my penis must have managed to have its own memory—and I entered Jennifer as quickly as I could before the whip cracked and horrible images stormed my mind.

My erection faded almost immediately. Jennifer tried to get me going. It was unbearable watching her from a thousand miles away. I put my hand on her head and whispered, stop. She rolled onto her back and looked at the ceiling, not breathing and then taking in the lightest wisp of air through her nose. I have never seen a human so alive yet so still.

What about me? she asked eventually. Then looked to the wall away from me. Is this ever going to end?

It's not that I don't want you. I actually suggested that they'd put too much potash or whatever in the bagged meals, and that maybe it would wear off. I put my arms around her, pulled her against me, and tried to console her, but it was like holding a giant bagged meal. She stuck with me for another year.

Stop, I ordered myself. Starlight from the window revealed the faint mass of the furniture in my bedroom in front of me. No reminiscing. A sudden snore-gasp came from Leo in the living room. I rolled onto my back and stared at the ceiling, taking in the lightest wisp of air through my nose.

In the morning, Leo groaned himself awake from the floor as I made tea. He seemed to expect me to serve his tea to him, which I did. When I last saw Leo, his business was starting to tank but he was still wealthy. Our mother's funeral. Funeral is not the right word. The state was collapsing around us and formal annexation had done nothing to slow it. Hers was one of the last cremations. We intended to scatter her ashes at the cabin with Dad's, but we couldn't get the gas to make the trip north.

Nice apartment, he said, leaning on an elbow and looking around.

Don't get any ideas.

You've taken neat to a whole new fucking level.

As you have slob.

He took a sip of his tea. Why did you come to Seattle anyway?

I brought the boys here after Jennifer died. We all needed a change of scene, and I thought Mom's relatives could help with the boys while I looked for work.

You never called. You never wrote. He mimicked a complaining mother.

Never did. I got out the fish food. Never called the rellies either. I fed the fish.

I didn't want to give him an opening, but I threw caution to the wind and asked what had happened to him since I last saw him.

Leo had always lived faster than anyone I knew. In grade six he sold fireworks; in high school he sold dope. He invested his earnings in stocks before he finished grade twelve. At university, while barely scraping through a degree in accountancy, he put together a stock deal that made millions. He moved to Seattle and invested in real estate. By age twenty, he had a yellow Corvette and partied hard six nights out of seven. A woman was sexually assaulted at a party at his place, but no charges were laid. Even when we knew for sure what was coming with climate change, even when everyone did, he was of the school that still wanted to take the planet out for one last, hard spin before trying to fix it. He was a let's-have-fun-and-go-out-in-a-wild-beautiful-explosion kind of guy. His philosophy distilled down to, Nothing lasts forever.

And yet he always knew to the dollar bill what his net worth was and to the minute what time it was. He knew the exact number of kilometres his Corvette had logged, how much money friends owed him, how far he'd jogged in the past week, how many calories he'd eaten that day.

Daytime, he lived in a rapid-fire world of numbers, nighttime, in a euphoric, somewhat paranoid, substance-induced whirlwind. I didn't see much of him after he moved to Seattle and Jennifer and I got married. He'd tried to get us to invest in a deal he was putting together, and tried to get our parents to as well, said we'd make a lot of money, and when we said no, he amped up the pressure. He went behind my back and tried to get Jennifer on board. When I confronted him he weaselled out, saying, *I was only trying to help*. If we had invested, we would have lost our shirts. Leo would probably have bailed us out but then we would have been beholden. I did not want to be beholden. My mother told me that a man had come looking for Leo and asked her how Leo made his money. Shortly after that Leo met and married Evie, an Australian working at a Tokyo chat bar. He got a job in a multinational life insurance company developing actuarial models for insurance against catastrophic weather events. He copyrighted his work and started his own business. Within five years, he was able to reveal that he was very, very rich. Evie and he had two girls as well as her son Griffin from a previous relationship.

Leo was unlucky in his parents. Our father, who adored the quasi-communal life of the army, might have accepted Leo's wealth if he'd kept it hidden, but he didn't know how to love a son who flaunted it, and our mother the high school English teacher was a socialist at heart. Leo was not someone I would have ever known if he wasn't my brother, but I always felt connected.

He put his empty teacup on the floor, sat up, wrapped the blanket around his shoulders, and leaned against the wall. He spoke loud enough I could hear him over the noise of stirring the porridge I was making for our breakfast.

I managed to take out enough cash for Evie and me and the girls before the shit really started hitting the fucking fan. Buried it in a safe in the garden. We moved our beds into the kitchen and only heated that room. I had no work to go to, so I hung around the house all day driving Evie nuts. She got me digging up the lawn so she could put in some vegetables. She made me teach the girls how to read and do math. One day she told me to take some cash and see if I could buy some live chickens. I ended up walking way too far—I was blown away by the changes in the city, you know what it was like—I just kept walking and didn't get back that night. I slept in a garden shed somewhere, woke up hungry, and ate some wormy apples. I went around knocking on the doors of houses where I smelled chickenshit, but no one wanted to trade the birds for cash. I slept out a second night and before dawn stole three chicks from one of the houses I'd visited.

I got depressed and just sat around watching Evie and the girls do all the work. She started giving me less and less food when she divvied up the dinner. I started to wander the city and sleep out more often, until finally I never went back.

The car you ticketed was stolen. I wanted to come and find you. I want to go to the cabin together. I've come to the end of myself.

I put in supplies for Jennifer, me, and the kids. Maybe they're still there.

Come with me, Allen. You've got nothing going on here. We'll take Mom's ashes up together. Maybe your boys will be there. We can fish and kill deer.

The deer population is depleted, and the island cougars, who are already the most aggressive on the continent, are starving. There are hardly any fish left. And what about vegetables, scurvy and such?

You always were a negative Nancy.

Transportation?

I can get us kayaks.

I laughed. I got dressed for work and handed him the apartment key. I held it in my hand over his palm—This is only for one day. Don't touch anything other than the fridge.

I was cold and hungry after work that night. I wondered where Leo had our mother's ashes, thinking I must ask him. The wind blew so hard it seemed it would strip the new buds off the trees, and the clouds were so thick that dusk was dark as night. I had to use my Callebaut.

No one knows how long these new flashlights are going to last, but they're definitely outlasting their owners. They were invented by a guy called Enstice Callebaut who discovered a way to isolate microscopic particles of nuclear waste, encase them safely, and convert them to light. Callebaut instantly became a hero and is honoured once a year on Guardians of the Future Day. A lesser star was the woman who found a way to wrangle wire coat hangers into devices to suspend the light from the headboards of beds, thereby expanding its radius and preserving the integrity of books' spines.

The flashlight gives off a cool, narrow line of illumination that has no glow. You have to point the beam directly in someone's face to make out their features, and no one wants that, so all we see of each other at night is our feet, unless the moon is out.

I fretted about what to feed Leo and decided to take him to the community dining hall.

When I opened my apartment door, Leo was sprawled in my armchair, using my mobile's precious daily charge. He wagged his index finger at me.

You've broken the rules, Allen. He nodded at the goldfish.

Mr Pure and Noble. Mr Saviour. Mr Enforcer. Mr Fucking Good of Mankind. I'm going to have to turn you in. I'm telling Mom.

Pets were outlawed in 2033 when it was deemed immoral to keep animals for pleasure while people starved and undomesticated species disappeared forever. I'd bought cartons of fish food, plastic bins to store it in, replacement tank lights, and filters. I'd found a black market supplier to replace fish at the cost of one week's pay. In their small, contained world, I could take care of them and do no harm. I could experience a sliver of love and appreciate their beauty—an easy pleasure, a tiny responsibility, a miniscule infraction. A life could only shrink so small without disappearing. I'd needed those fish to survive.

I flushed with annoyance. Get off my mobile.

Where'd you get them? He put my mobile down with elaborate care on the side table. Hunt's Point? Medina? South Tacoma? Capitalism creeping in on the margins, eh?

Why are you using my mobile when I told you not to touch anything?

Allen, my brother, take a load off. Let me get you a drink.

I don't drink anymore.

No shit. Wishful thinking. A cup of tea then?

I sat down in my easy chair, and he spoke to me like the master of my own kitchen.

I'm sorry about the mobile, but I was so fucking bored and I didn't feel like reading *War and Peace*. He made air quotes. I mean, where did you get such singularly uninteresting books? That takes a special talent.

I owned three unreturned library books: *War and Peace*, *Brecht: A Biography*, and *A Distant Mirror: The Calamitous 14th Century*. There were four books from our parents' library: *Bad Dirt*, *The Intelligent Woman's Guide to Socialism and Capitalism*, *Learn French the Fast and Fun Way*, *Weekend Woodworking with Power Tools—18 Quick and Easy Projects*, and two of my sons' old classics, *Charlie and the Chocolate Factory* and *Harry Potter and the Philosopher's Stone*.

Leo yawned, I wanted to find out what was happening in the world. It's been a while.

You truly live like a bum then?

Bum is a bit insensitive. There are places. Dormitories.

He gave me back my mobile. I checked the history and asked, what's Occupy Now Gold Chat?

Some buddies from the old days. Haven't seen them in years. I was mildly curious what they were up to. He got the milk out of the coolbox.

What happened with the leg? He nodded toward my prosthesis.

Garbage truck ran over it after Jennifer and I split. I don't remember much. I was passed out beside a dumpster.

Mom and Dad would be so proud.

Yeah. We're starting to make quite a pair.

We began laughing, and every time we looked at each other, laughed harder. Leo carried a kitchen chair and placed it beside the easy chair and brought in two cups of tea.

So, seriously, Leo. *Are* you looking to get yourself killed?

He looked away.

You know mobs have killed people for less?

He shrugged. I'm not sure more life is what the doctor's ordering right now. He smiled thinly. I am bored. So bored I can barely be bothered to feed myself. Fatally bored. You know me, I don't like having to cooperate and play nicely with the other assholes in the sandbox. I want to grab everything for myself and then not even play with it. Just savour knowing other people want it. It's the way I am.

He was getting back in his armour. His eyes weren't settling on anything.

Hence my mobile, I observed.

He glanced at me, then raised one hand as though he were a king graciously bestowing a gift.

One of the last pleasures of a dying man.

Those could add up, I had a feeling.

We finished our tea in silence.

I replayed Ruby's presence in the room. It was radioactive. I crossed my legs to hide an erection.

I told Leo that the government had announced another amnesty period. All he had to do was turn himself in and he'd get set up with a housing unit, a job, a Callebaut, and a mobile. I offered to take him by the office the next morning. He said sure, sure, and asked if I had a woman.

Something about his asking put me on edge. I didn't feel like sharing my sandbox toys.

Why, did someone come by?

He smiled.

Did she leave a message?

Not really. We had a good conversation though. Interesting woman.

Leo, I am going to help you out of your misery right now and permanently, if you don't tell me word for word what she said.

A tactical error, I knew immediately, but there was no right move. I remembered the ease with which Ruby had taken her clothes off. I replayed the way Leo was sprawled in my armchair when I got home. His talk about boredom, the last pleasures of a dying man. Still, I doubted he would have laughed the way we did at the thought of our parents seeing us if he'd just poached my woman. Then I didn't doubt it.

I leaned forward in my chair, hunting thoughts in his eyes. He looked back at me with a defiant glitter, then he crumpled. I will always be the one who had what he wanted and now can never have. And I have never really wanted anything he had. I realize now, writing this, that that picture of himself in the sandbox, just having all the toys and not even playing with them, is how he saw me in our family.

She was looking for you, obviously. I offered her tea but she didn't want anything. When I told her I was your brother, she asked me some questions about what kind of kid you were, where we grew up. That kind of thing.

I didn't want Leo to know I had no way to reach her. I didn't want Leo to know anything about her. I wanted to make sure he never set eyes on her again. And I was thrilled she had come looking for me.

Where'd you meet a woman like that? he asked.

I don't want to talk about it.

It's not hard to see why you'd want to keep her all to yourself.

I remained silent.

Allen, give me some money for booze. Don't worry, I'll fuck off soon, but I have to have a drink tonight.

I bought him a half-litre of rye on the way to the dining hall. During dinner we asked about each other's families to fill in the time. Leo said he used to walk by his old house and listen for their voices, but when the garden had been silent for a while, he stopped going by. He hadn't had the courage to look inside.

It dawned on me to feel guilty that I never tried to contact my nieces. Luke and Sam used to bug me to visit their cousins, then they stopped. Leo and I forked our lasagne in. It had been a kind of madness not to think about my nieces during such dangerous times. I saw those two little girls with their pink ATVs and their big-screen TVs, their pom-poms and purses.

I got unnerved amid the clatter and talk in the cafeteria. Leo asked about Sam and Luke. He latched onto them as a subject. And I thought, why is he worrying about my sons instead of his daughters?

Allen, did you ever think they might have gone to the cabin? Did they ever talk to you about it?

Like I said, I was planning on taking the family there when things got really bad. The boys were young then, but they probably knew.

Allen. Let's go. Let's go up there. Let's see if they're there.

What about your daughters?

They might be there too.

I looked down at his empty plate and spoke slowly.

If the boys survived, they're probably fine. If I start worrying about my sons, I will not be able to stay sane. My world is not big enough for that. They don't need my shame. And I don't need their forgiveness.

Leo was scanning the cafeteria.

Next morning, he was gone when I woke up.

I checked if Leo had taken anything, then fed my fish as my tea was brewing and my porridge was setting. I watched them eat while I ate and drank. The males have longer, lighter-coloured feathery fins, while the females are rounder, bigger, and more efficient. Three of the fish darted with golden brilliance after the desiccated flakes drifting down past the plastic plants to the treasure chest with skull and crossbones that Luke gave me, but the fourth fish, a male, remained hovering near the bottom. I tapped the glass beside the fourth fish with my spoon. It spurted forward a bit, keeled over, then righted itself. They never get better. I tapped again and the sick fish shimmied slowly up to take a few unconvincing bites of a flake on the surface. One of the other fish swam over and jerked the flake away.

The sick fish sank back to the bottom. I finished my porridge. The sick fish depressed me. I washed my spoon and bowl and went to take another sip of tea when, out of the corner of my eye, I saw the sick goldfish give a sudden jerk. Two of the others had muscled into its corner behind the plastic plants and—I saw it—one of them swam up to the sick one and took a bite out of its fin. The sick fish jerked again and moved a couple of centimetres forward.

I sprang into action. I got more food and tried to fob the sons of bitches off with extra flakes. The new food distracted them for a minute or two, but then they closed in again. The sick one flapped its tail and moved a few centimetres as they approached.

My father used to say that only man is truly cruel because he has free will and is conscious of what he does. He said only man kills for fun. I wish he could see this. Try to imagine, I'd like to say to him, two men, stuffed to the gills, so to speak, so definitely *not* hungry, taking nibbles off a dying man—biting off an occasional toe or ear lobe, unaffected by his cries of pain. They wouldn't be *abnormal* men, I'd explain to my father in a deadpan tone, just regular, everyday guys.

I filled a glass bowl with water, matching the temperature as best I could to the tank's water, and got out my green fish net. I should've just flushed the sick one down the toilet. Without a miracle from the fish god—who never seems to dish out miracles—it was going to die. But because this tiny brainless flash of orange was my pet, I felt responsible for it.

I lowered the net into the tank. The sick fish scurried through the plants to the opposite side. The healthy ones also fled. Piscatory helter-skelter. After a couple of passes and a flick of my wrist, I caught the sick one and transferred it to the bowl. I picked out a sprig of fake greenery so the invalid would feel at home and sprinkled in a few flakes, in case it wanted to eat before going belly up.

Experience has taught me that there is no green net in life. I have only seen the opposite. When the other fish in your tank attack, you need your own army to survive, no matter how many representatives you have at the UN or OneWorld's Regional Council.

I scrubbed the green net gently using dish detergent and a nail brush, rinsed it thoroughly with water from my rainwater bucket, dried it first with a towel, then by waving it in the air, and returned it to its place in the utensil drawer. By the time I pushed the drawer shut, the tremors had come on and I had to get to work.

I was tired that day. Leo's visit had drained me, but when I handed my scanner back to Velma and hung up my uniform jacket, I got a surge. Ruby! I checked the time on my mobile, thought it must be about the same as the last two times I'd met her. I lounged against the stone wall like a man with nothing to do but wait for a woman. I picked out the sound of her heels from a distance and waited with a silly grin. I invited her for dinner.

I live in an old office building near the original railway yard. It was converted to apartments at the turn of the century. Its front entrance has been boarded shut and a small door fitted inside the old one to minimize heat loss. I unlocked the door and held it open for her. We still had just enough daylight to make our way up the three flights of stairs with me touching the wall and leading the way. I got my key out of my pocket and lifted it to the keyhole. The air in the hallway seemed suddenly sucked away and a shyness came over me, which I tried to hide. I unlocked the door to my apartment, switched on the light, and held the door open.

What a pauper's gesture! Come in to my garden of earthly delight, my nest, lovingly built to attract a mate. I had never really seen my apartment until this moment. Other than the one coat hook, I had taken no steps to make it home. There were no curtains, no pictures, no vases or trinkets or photographs. The place was the civilian version of a barracks. I also smelled it for the first time, the heretofore invisible scent of self, like the smell of clothes brought out of storage—the musty skin oils that laundering never quite removes. The overall ambience would not be helped by the goldfish, now floating belly-up in the glass bowl beside the kitchen sink, luckily mostly hidden by a tall jar of oats.

Ruby ducked under my arm. Of course she'd already seen my apartment, but not formally, not by invitation, not with my conscious awareness. I followed her in, went directly to the living room window, and opened it. I invited her to sit in the stuffed chair, grabbed Leo's bedding from the corner, took it into the bedroom, and shoved it in the closet. I had the thought of changing the locks; he was the kind of guy who would get a key copied. Then I picked up the glass bowl, holding it in front of me so my body blocked her sightline, and rushed it to the bathroom. I poured the contents into the toilet, briefly admired the beauty of my fish, and flushed, but the water pressure was too low to push even a raisin down the pipe.

I went back to the kitchen for a soup ladle. Ruby was crouching in front of the shelf under the windows, looking through my micro library. Her jacket had fallen open. She wore a slip of sky blue silk—an arresting garment in these times. Its shimmer reminded me of the fish's scales.

Just be a minute, I said, and disappeared back into the bathroom where I spooned the fish out of the toilet bowl back into the glass bowl and, for lack of any better place, hid it under my bed. I came back out and put the kettle on, closed the window, put the soup ladle in a pot to sanitize later, plugged the heater into my battery, set it in front of her, and asked if she was hungry. Before she answered I went to the coolbox, opened the door and announced, egg, sausage, and toast on the menu tonight.

She was back in the armchair, feet up on the ottoman, immersed in a book she'd chosen from the shelf. That blue silk clung to her. Starved, she said. Are you a decent cook? You don't mind if I read while you work?

I can find my way around a frying pan. Read. More peace for the chef.

I was glad of the chance to get used to her presence without having to talk. I lay the sausages in the frying pan with a sizzle and stared out the window while they cooked, then broke the eggs into the pan and watched the tide of white move from the edges to the vortex.

She had ravaged me the last time and there was a predatory aspect to her now, like our family cat who used to pretend to sleep in the backyard while birds hopped closer.

I forked the sausages onto two plates, and the egg and toast, and called madam to dinner. I had one hand on the back of a kitchen chair while the other hung by my side, fluttering, as though I were playing alternating notes on a piano with my thumb and baby finger. She looked at that hand and lay the book down.

We sat at the table watching the goldfish while we ate. I berated myself for offering her dinner. It was much more awkward than just having sex. At least she was hungry. She ate voraciously.

Do you come from a large family? I inquired.

No. She took another bite and asked with her mouth full, Why?

73

Usually people who eat that fast had to compete for seconds.

No, I was an only child. I guess I just like to get to my pleasures fast.

I choked and laughed at the same time.

It was then I asked about her, where she grew up, that kind of thing. She gave me the thin version. A résumé.

I'm from Bellingham, former Washington State. Only child, older parents, both dead. Before the die-off I was a custom's officer at the Peace Arch/Blaine border crossing. I did that for seven years. It got tough when people started trying to move north and the Canadians made us turn everyone back. The job got a lot better after annexation and all we had to do was direct people to the nearest resources. When OneWorld came into play I could've switched to doing city borders, but a lot of folks wanted that gig and I was done. I travelled for a couple of years, then I started performing. I sing and dance now to cover my rations and such. Though I could use a larger food ration.

It wasn't hard to notice what was not being said. *I travelled for a couple of years.* What that would have meant for a lone woman in the early days of OneWorld. And then the next thirteen years—*I sing and dance to cover my rations.* I sensed a fellow loner marching with oblivion's band, yet she seemed also to be facing forward, taking risks the way I used to. I admired her. She finished eating and lay her fork and knife neatly across the centre of her plate, pushed her chair out from the table, and tilted it back on two legs.

I looked up. The widest point of her face was just below where her eyes were. Her brows were dark and defined.

The last time someone looked at me, Allen Quincy, the way she did, was ... never. I felt like a package being opened with an exacto knife.

She took my hand and led me to my own bedroom. She undressed me and then undressed herself. Her eyes were filled with light. She pulled me down to my bed and helped take off my prosthesis and put her lips to my stump and kissed it. Every nuance of movement between us seemed to spark another nuance. The feeling of skin, naked skin, was like waking up from a dream.

Next morning I woke up first. She was still in the bed beside me. It was my day off, it was Sunday, we could go to a teahouse, I could treat her to something. I was thinking maybe I could pull this off, this romance thing. I felt fine.

Usually I would have caught up on the news, maybe doubled up on my daily calisthenics, washed the laundry and hung it out if it wasn't raining. I would've spent the afternoon at the library, come home, made dinner, and gone to bed.

Instead I doubled up on the porridge and tea and served madam in bed. She was strong, wiry, and hungry—a perfect combination of satiation and desire. A deep burn ignited in me, holding her that morning.

We stepped out together. The wind was up, the temperature suddenly warmer, warm for winter, even now, and the sky was brown. We could taste the dust from the Great Plains

Desert a thousand kilometres to the east. Fine sand piled up in small drifts. We bent over to avoid the sting on our faces, held our coats closed, and pushed forward toward a new establishment announced in the news banners. We stopped under the viaduct for relief from the dust and wind. Our clothes and hair were covered. I blew sand out of Ruby's eyelashes and she did the same for me.

I pointed out the putty-coloured man. She smiled and ran over to another painting of a window frame with fish swimming through it, placed one hand as though on the ledge, and turned and faced the fish so they seemed to be about to swim around her.

I can't believe it, I said. I'm standing here with Mary Poppins in a sidewalk chalk drawing.

She pirouetted over to the giant, so that the large figure looked down at her with one eye and up at her with the other one.

Who's Mary Poppins? This is excellent down here, Quincy. This one's like Humpty Dumpty, but he's not sure he wants to get back up on that wall. Who's painting them? Where do they get the paint?

We walked back out into the driving airborne desert and continued forward. When we passed the old post office, we saw there was some kind of new indoor market happening. Plastic sheeting was tacked up over the broken windows near the ceiling, and it snapped and cracked like a rodeo whip in the wind. We went inside and wandered down the aisles, Hump and Stump and Twinkletoes, and looked at all the stalls where people sold or traded clothes, crockery, kitchen ware, home-brewed beer, baked goods, dried herbs, teas, home gadgetry, wood-working.

Ruby started to get excited. Flowers! Scones! She pulled me over to a stall. Look at this dress! I could create a piece around this. She smelled the armpits and crinkled her face. I don't own enough perfume to cover that. She turned it inside out looking for a label. McQueen, she whispered to herself. How much? The woman in the stall turned around and looked Ruby up and down. She was missing two teeth. A mole near the corner of her mouth had sprouted several long hairs. She touched the hem of the garment lightly, gently rubbing the fabric between her thumb and forefinger, a slight tremor revealing itself when her hand stilled.

A movie star wore that exact same dress. One of the exotics. Was it Tilda Swinton?

Is it washable?

I don't know. You can have it. A gift. The woman looked at me and winked. The only clothes I could imagine getting excited about when it came to Ruby was no clothes, but I was glad she was happy.

Ruby's manner, usually so direct and self-possessed, had changed. A girlish side had surfaced. It was sweet but overdone and strained—like a daughter trying too hard to charm her father, not manipulatively but because she loves him and doesn't know how else to connect. It surprised and touched me. As we walked together she began to dash about, exclaiming over everything and returning, eyes sparkling, putting her hands on my sleeve. I began to feel like a crab with a kitten.

I stopped walking and pretended to brush her hair out of her face, looking deep into her eyes to get past the bubbly manner. She was in there, looking out at me, uncertain, excited, on the edge of being happy. I pulled her to me and kissed her there, among the hurly burly, and she stilled for the duration of the kiss, but when it ended she ran over to a table of fresh herbs.

At the far end of the hall a line-up had formed. I asked a woman standing with her young daughter, who was dressed in some kind of ratty ballet dress, what the line-up was for. Ice cream! I couldn't believe it. It was like hearing Ruby's high heels. Years had gone by without ice cream. I told Ruby, You keep exploring and I'll buy us ice cream cones. If they have flavours, what would you like?

She looked around her and suddenly shrank into herself. It's too much, she said. Let's leave. She pulled at my wrist. I scanned the room for anything that might have set her off.

You're sure you don't want an ice cream cone? After all these years? The line's moving pretty fast. We might never get another one.

She stared straight ahead at my shirt button. I put my arm around her and we left.

She knocked on my apartment door around nine the next night, complaining about the dark stairwell. She was still wearing the blue silk dress. We went straight to the bedroom. We undressed and she pulled me down on the bed. The sight of one another was like rocket fuel. Neither of us were the sort to delay satisfaction.

Afterward she lay in my arms, where I'd gathered her, my chin on her head. She raised her head off the pillow and sniffed.

It stinks in here. Like fish, and not fresh fish either.

Instant shame. You can't smell your own smell. Should I have taken the sheets to the laundry? With Leo here, and the suddenness of this love affair, I hadn't had time to plan out domestic details. My nose was in her hair, and all I could smell was the cedar perfume of her shampoo. I raised my head and sniffed. The odour was like tide pools after a day in the baking sun or two-day dead crab. It was clinging to the paint on the walls, circulating through the air pockets in the mattress, permeating the curtains. I got up and investigated. It wasn't coming from the kitchen, outside, or from the apartments above or below.

Then I remembered. I crouched down beside the bed and fished out the bowl. The goldfish's belly was very swollen now and its eyes filmy and sunken. I strapped on my leg, pulled on my pants, my shoe, a shirt, winked at her—Let me handle this, little lady—and exited with the bowl.

I carried it downstairs and outside. Every year, when the new buds are about to unfurl into leaves, the city drapes the trees with fine netting to protect them from burning in the sun. In the moonlight the street looked like a ghostly sculpture garden. I walked over to the base of one of the trees. The square of earth in the sidewalk was covered with dead leaves and bits of twig. The goldfish's body, lacerated at the gills and whitened around the mouth and tail, flashed out of the bowl, like a thought that slipped someone's mind, and nose-dived into the leaves. It should have slipped from sight and rotted under the leaves except that it seemed to meet some sort of obstacle, so the tail stuck out, creating the surreal impression that the dead fish was burrowing into a hole or trying to reach a morsel of food under the leaves.

Even outside the smell was strong. I worried a raccoon or stray cat that had survived the crises against all odds would eat it and become sick. Surely evolution had taught everything but true scavengers to stay away from rotten fish, but instincts can be massively imperfect in their ability to protect a species. As we know.

Allen, I said to myself, the universe must take responsibility for itself. In the narrow light of my Callebaut I saw a black beetle tentatively approach the fish's diving cadaver. It reached out and caressed the bright scales with its antennae and thread-like feet. And it was the caressing which was the problem, which sucked me down a funnel. That dead goldfish seemed to have become a focal point for a reawakening tenderness in me. Ruby had softened me up. A suppressed memory, thin like the beetle's leg, tested my edges to see if I was defended or inert, to see if I was vulnerable or ready to turn with savage jaw and bite back. It was the quality of the goldfish flesh, its not-too-springy plumpness, like the turkeys my mother pressed with her forefinger to see if they were fresh, that dulled golden flesh being caressed by the ever-so-thin tip of a beetle's leg. An image streaked across my mind of flesh, cold and blue in death, streaked by a thin line of blood dissolving in rain.

My diaphragm plummeted, creating a vacuum that forced me to suck in air with such intensity that I barked. Several violent involuntary inhalations followed.

I turned and made my way slowly, stiff and brittle now, no more the thirty-year-old lover, back to my apartment. Ruby was in the armchair wearing an old sweater of mine and her dancing tights. She looked at me with narrowed eyes and a grin.

Jeez, you sure know how to make a girl feel self-conscious.

A laugh escaped me. I washed the bowl and scrubbed the sink. Scrubbed my hands. I asked if she wanted tea or something to eat. She said she'd make tea, and I sat on the arm of the chair and watched her move around the kitchen. I walked up behind her, pressed my erection into her hip and ... even the cannibal goldfish began to blush.

Later, when we were sipping our tea, she in the armchair and me on a kitchen chair, our legs touching on the ottoman, I felt relieved enough to ask, You met my brother the other day?

I did.

He mentioned you asked about me. What did he tell you?

He said you used to be different. Confident. Self-righteous. Adventurous. You were a colonel or major something. He barely recognized you now, he said.

That goes both ways. Was he, I paused, a gentleman?

What do you mean? Did he offer me his chair? A glass of water? Did he make a pass? He was charming, as I imagine you'd expect your brother to be. He was curious. He grilled me about us.

Unavoidably. I'm curious too.

He mentioned a cabin up north. A family cabin that he wants you to go to with him. He wanted me to convince you.

I don't know why he wants to go so much.

He said your mother's ashes. And he thinks he could survive up there. He said he's not doing so well down here. Is he your older brother?

Younger.

He seemed like the older one. The way he sat in your chair and opened your coolbox.

I haven't seen him in eighteen years.

You don't look like brothers.

We both have our mother's blue eyes and our father's big hands.

One short, one tall, one thick, one thin, one hairy, one hairless ...

Clearly there was no way of finding out if anything happened between them without asking directly. I didn't think that would go over well so instead I continued the list of contrasts she'd started.

One devastatingly handsome, smart, and good, the other ...

I got up and made two sandwiches with the cheese and solar greenhouse lettuce and tomato we'd got at the market. I had a small jar of mustard and I splurged. Ruby clapped her hands she was so happy.

I haven't eaten this well—I can't even remember.

I wanted to tell you about the goldfish.

She nodded and kept eating.

I'm not normally a rule breaker. I fully support OneWorld. I don't even want to go back to the old world, unlike my brother.

She nodded vigorously, her mouth full of sandwich.

I made the decision to keep my fish a long time ago, and then I stopped thinking about the rule. You know how things can become invisible until someone else sees them? I wouldn't keep a cat or a dog.

She swallowed and waited.

I'm thinking I won't replace them when the last one dies.

We all need something, one thing, that's just for us, she said, free of rules and other people. No rule would stop me from dancing.

She left sometime after midnight. I offered to accompany her but she said she liked walking by herself. I gave her my Callebaut so she'd have to return it.

She came over every night that week. I didn't question it. I gratefully accepted. We threw ourselves at each other, trying to get under each other's skin through the calisthenics of desire and love. I say love. It wasn't the love of twenty-year-olds—we'd both already had good helpings of life—nor was it the love of commitment and sacrifice yet, but I would already have given up a lot for her. Sometimes we made love with so much frustration and fear and uncertainty that we bashed ourselves against each other, and these times might have been the most lustful.

She started staying the night, leaving with me in the morning when I went to work. I noticed something about her. She was often still, and by still I mean stiller than anyone I'd ever met. She didn't fiddle, or tap or move her head, or rearrange any part of her posture. She found her position and committed to it. Lizard still. Or she was moving. When I cooked I'd glance at her and she'd have a leg up on the counter, leaning forward in a stretch, or she'd have her leg back and be pulling her foot toward her head, or she'd throw one arm over her shoulder and clasp it with the other hand.

I had push-up grips on the floor, which protected my wrists, and she'd drop to them almost carelessly and float a quick thirty or forty push-ups and then float to something else.

As a soldier who had gone through boot camp and several reboot camps, whose body was trained to take punishment and stay effective in extreme situations, watching the way Ruby inhabited her body was like watching a slightly different species. I felt like a robot or some sort of automaton next to her, except when we were making love, and then my body seemed miraculously to know the same language.

I wanted to know more about her. How did you become a dancer? I asked. She had a way of answering that was precise but deflecting, keeping me at a distance. Her parents had been people with jobs, she said. First-generation immigrants: mother Portuguese, father Argentinian. They wanted a career for her, an education, a step up the ladder—doctor, lawyer, pharmacist. She remembered, even when she was a toddler, making up dances to the music they played—Fado, tango, gypsy, hip hop, classical—and then practicing the moves over and over. She'd asked for dance lessons, but they kept putting her off. Finally, when she was eight years old, they agreed to pay for one lesson a week, but she knew she wanted to become a great dancer and to do that she'd have to train every day. She arranged to work as a receptionist for her ballet teacher after school and on weekends in exchange for classes five days a week. She did this from age eight to thirteen, when she tore her hamstring.

I prodded more. So how is it you became a customs officer?

I left home at seventeen, she said. I was restless and wanted to be independent and free of rules. I got a job at a mall and couldn't afford lessons anymore. I fell in love. Etcetera. My boyfriend's mother had a connection at the border and the pay was much better.

In the morning when we went our separate ways, I asked where she was going. She was never one to volunteer information. My day to lead dance class, she answered and turned down a different street, bundled up in layers of sweaters and tights.

Why did you pick me? I asked one evening after dinner, feeling playful.

Didn't you pick me?

No. I only offered myself.

Are you fishing for compliments?

Of course.

A smile took over her face, starting in her eyes, which softened from the focus of eating, a focus that was singular and intense with her, and slowly spread to a grin.

Your eyes, she said. The way they're set in your face. You could meet me in the middle of a riot or an earthquake, and you'd still be looking at me.

She ran her finger over her plate to get the last bit of juice from the sausages. Your muscles. Then licked her finger. And the fact that you're not desperately trying to survive, but you're not defeated either. It's true you seem a bit dead, but a girl's not worth her salt if she doesn't like a bit of a challenge.

I laughed.

The only truly sexy thing in this world, Allen Quincy, is consciousness and you, despite the partly dead bit, have that in spades.

Any thoughts of keeping my life small and controlled went out the window. I parked my brain, double-parked my past, jacked up disbelief, and towed skepticism to the

wrecking yard. Whether she had been created by a benev-
olent universe or by luck to save me, I didn't care; she was
in my bed and she was resurrecting me toe by toe, follicle
by follicle, scar by scar.

If I had only accepted what she offered without seeking
more, we might have been all right.

Earlier this evening, I used my penknife to break the seal on the whiskey bottle and therefore had to go looking for it when I needed to sharpen my pencil. I found myself pouring another drink, though I had not intended to, knocked it back in three gulps, and now I'm over the line. My pencil may be sharp but my mind is too dull to keep my story going. There'll be no laying an ambush tonight.

I have a confession, besides that I'm drunk.

I'm ashamed to admit it and have never revealed this to anyone.

I think I am a good man.

Still.

We always said, We're fighting for peace, we're risking our lives so others can live in peace. They sell every war as a vaccination against a future one, a prophylaxis against itself—have one now so you won't need a bigger one later. But that *is* why I became a soldier. I loved the camaraderie and not being behind a desk, and there was my father, but really I became a soldier because I wanted to stand up for innocent civilians against the bad guys ...

Maybe I was a good man, who knows. In any case, once again I am a man who can no longer live with himself.

Now my pencil is dull too. I'm going to sleep.

It was around that time I started having one of those re-
peating dreams, and one morning before we got out of bed,
I told her about it.

I locked you up in a gingerbread house in a cage beside
the oven and I was fattening you up. I was feeding you roast
chicken and gravy and beef—feasts from the old days—tan-
doori, teriyaki, cookies, puddings, trifles, and cakes. I kept
them coming, feeding you through an opening in your cage.
All the time I had the key to your cage, a chicken bone on
a strip of rawhide, around my neck.

I didn't tell her that in the dream she was naked and
scared and cringed in the corner of the cage except when
I brought her food.

You ate like a wild animal, stuffing your face until the
food was gone, but you never put on any weight and I worried I might never be able to eat you.

She laughed. It wasn't a full laugh—it was short, a sound
of surprise and pleasure in the surprise.

That's quite a flattering picture you paint of yourself, she
said, a wicked witch in a gingerbread house. She stretched
out under the covers, put her arm across my chest, and
whispered, I better be careful tonight when I'm eating so
you don't discover where I'm putting it all. I want to keep
you working hard in that kitchen.

I went to work that day feeling happy, though I see now,
also with an undertone of anxiety. I had never thought I'd
feel happy in that way again. Connected to someone. The
rain had stopped and it was silent outside except for a light

gurgling of water in drainpipes. I took the longer route by the bay where the loading docks used to be, wanting to stretch out my walk. The huge red loading cranes stood in water up to their knees, like a phalanx of long-necked robot Apatasauri, lifting their heads as though at a sound and looking into the distance.

A skateboarder tattooed at speed toward me and I had to spin away to avoid getting knocked over. The kid hurtled past, hair sticking out from his grey wool toque, toting a backpack big enough to hold all he owned. He might have been fifteen or sixteen, my youngest son's age when he and his brother left.

Because I was happy and letting my guard down, I let myself think, just for a flash, about Jennifer and Luke and Sam. All the love was there, like an ocean stretching forever, deep blue, sparkling and fierce. I glanced out over the expanse, but even that instant of opening brought with it a howling clamour, a gnashing and tearing. I broke into a sweat and fled toward work.

Velma said I looked like I'd seen my own ghost and uncharacteristically shared some hot tea from her thermos.

A few days later Ruby kicked my door rather than knocking on it. She stood in the hallway, hands cupped in front, holding salmonberries. First of the season. A bit sour, but still. She let them fall onto the kitchen counter then fed us, one for her, one for me.

We were getting exhausted from lack of sleep and the intensity of the preceding nights so we decided to snack on leftovers in bed and read. Ruby had to make sure there were enough leftovers before she agreed to forgo dinner.

Her mobile was always undercharged because she barely ever went home, so we scanned the news together on mine. Headline: The Council of Armed Conflict Arrests over a Thousand on Three Continents. The rebels, organized in a network of cells, are planning to gain control of resource-rich regions in isolated areas. They have succeeded in building up weapons caches—though how many is still unknown. They have gone undetected by using an agricultural language code over long-range, solar-charged two-way radios. Anyone noticing suspicious behaviour consistent with such activities is asked to report it immediately. The Council reiterates that the global environment is still too volatile to allow for any deregulated activities, and that this subversive network's success could imperil everyone.

I handed the mobile to Ruby with the comment, It's surprising how little time it takes for some people to get over their fear of extinction. I opened a book.

She scanned for a while then lay back and looked up at the ceiling. In school, she eventually said, I remember learning that the motion of the tiniest particle of matter can change just from the force of being looked at. Quincy, what do you suppose happens when all the particles that go into making a human being collide into each other the way we have?

Ruby told me not to expect her for a few days. She kept it vague. Something for her work.

The first night alone, I came home from work and changed into my slippers and army sweater. I made tea and got my mobile ready on the side table. After so much sex, I expected to feel relaxed and pleasantly tired. I was looking forward to reading the news at length and at my own pace.

They have a hard time keeping the news upbeat these days. Their desperation can be funny, for example today's banner, Lost Girl Found With Mystery Animal, showed a wet, dirty eight-year-old with a fluffy tan creature perched on her shoulder, clearly a stuffed gopher. This was followed by East Coast Shelters Overwhelmed Again, and Global Temperature Rise Only 0.1 Celsius in 6 Months. I scrolled down: New Strain of Dysentery Kills 100,000 in Central Africa; Food Production, Water Use, and Population to Balance by 2057 with One-Child Law.

I read for a while, sipping my tea, but then I looked up, and everything in my apartment irritated me. The walls were stained and the drywall chipped, the join between the floor and the baseboards was uneven, and the finish in the corners lumpy. I heard the kid upstairs running up and down the hall and rain pinging loudly on metal where the drainpipe was broken. Someone brushed their hands over my door as they felt their way up the creaking stairs to their apartment.

My apartment felt thin and cheap and badly built. I no longer felt hidden and pleasantly dormant in my home. Everywhere I looked I saw Ruby out of the corner of my eye. I began pacing inside my head, back and forth, back and forth. What was she doing to me? I'd been coping. I had my pleasures. I did my work. I was off the booze. I had my mind tamped down.

Now she was getting on with her life—visiting an old friend, staging a new choreography, sleeping god knows where—she hadn't specified when she'd be back, and I was beginning to come undone.

I hadn't understood what was happening to me. I'd thought, if I thought at all, that she was bringing me back to life but I hadn't thought what coming back to life would really mean. For the three nights she wasn't there, Ruby was like a mirror, angled to reflect the longest, darkest corridors inside me. This was when I thought—I am going to pay for this.

No woman wants a man who can't live without her. I was determined to conceal that I found her absence unbearable.

The third night the empty echo started to recede. I bought myself sausage and spud for dinner to cook with some old cabbage and dried herbs. I'd gone off my fitness routine earlier because of a tweak in my back, but I started again with renewed vanity. I came home, changed into gym strip, and did three sets of push-ups, crunches, doorway chin-ups, and weight-reps followed by joint mobilizations. I showered, then cooked up the sausages, sliced them into discs, and mixed them with the boiled potatoes, cabbage, some oil, and the herbs. I fed my remaining goldfish with no less affection, despite their intra-pisco sadism, and cracked open the book I'd been rereading before she showed up, the biography of Bertolt Brecht, six or seven years overdue at the library. I propped the book up against the wall, wedged it in place with a rock I use for the purpose, and started to fork in my dinner as the fish twinkled in their tank, snatching at swirling flakes of food. I savoured the bursts of salty sausage with the bland potatoes and slightly crunchy cabbage. I was near the end of the book, after Brecht had died, and the author explained how Brecht wanted to be buried in a steel coffin because he had a horror of being eaten by worms.

An expensive, bulletproof coffin seemed out of character for the playwright, a committed Marxist, he of the philosophy, All that is solid melts into air. Why insist on spending a small fortune to deprive worms of a meal that would have been no skin off his back, so to speak? Hadn't anyone told him that the worms would be going into the coffin with him, already latent in the bubbly soup of his bowels? He had specified too that he wanted to be buried with a stiletto in his heart. I was sorting out that a stiletto probably meant a knife and not the spike heel of a woman's shoe and pondering how such a thing could be "placed" in someone's heart, when a rap followed by a shuffle in front of my apartment door caused my heart to leap like a schoolgirl's.

I tossed my fork onto my plate, pushed back my chair, and rushed to open the door. Her hair was plastered to her skull, her face was flushed, and she wore a strange new garment made of gray rags stitched to some kind of flesh-coloured bodice with the red shoes and her customs-uniform jacket. She stepped into the apartment and looked around. Where before she had been in charge, spectacularly so, now she seemed timid, apprehensive, hunted. The apartment was warmer than usual with the heat from the cooker and the body heat from my exercises. She took off her coat and held it folded over her hands. I took it from her and put it on the hook over mine. She was covered in sweat and her lean muscles bulged.

Are you all right? I asked.

She turned and looked at me, recharging before my eyes. She put her hand against my chest and backed me up against the closed front door, took my shoulders, turned us around so she was against the door, and wrapped one leg around my hips. The rest of this "pirouette" will stay locked in the memory bank.

After her spirited rally, Ruby slumped again. I gave her a plate of leftovers and she received it like a beggar getting a handout. She ate warily, looking up frequently—at the goldfish, at me, at the cover of my book. I got up and placed a glass in front of her. I got a bottle of whiskey, bought specially for her, out from under the sink and broke the seal.

Thank you.

You're welcome.

I carried her plate to the sink. You changed your dress.

You're not joining me? she asked, raising her glass.

Can't.

I reached over and caressed her cheek with the back of my hand. She leaned into the caress, then took a deep breath and sat back.

Why not?

I sat down across from her.

I am not being evasive, but I'm so very tired of myself. I'll tell you sometime, if you're still curious, but I just don't feel like talking about myself. I am happy to see *you*.

She looked down at her hands lying in her lap. When people look down at their hands like that, it's a submission.

It's quite possible that I'm tired of myself too.

I pushed the glass closer to her.

I wish I could sing right now, I said to her.

Then I did something extraordinary, for me. I sang the only song I could think of, "Twinkle, Twinkle, Little Star." My voice cracked and slid out of tune. Tears came to her eyes and then she began to cry in earnest. She grabbed my hand and held it to her cheek.

I had a daughter once, she said to the air in front of her. Ruby's skin was hot now. She fought the tears back down, lost. A short wail escaped her lips, then she fought again, turning her mouth to my hand and biting my knuckle.

She got sick and died when things were at their worst, just before OneWorld came into being. She was only six.

I think it was at this moment I wondered how, after nineteen years of celibacy and solitude, it would be this woman who tempted me out. It was the way she strode down the street in those red heels, ready to take what she wanted without apology, yet not wanting to take anything. There was something wild about her, but ravaged too, fierce but broken, hot but drowning. It was sex, but really it was what fuelled the sex.

I had tried dating once or twice after Jennifer and I split, but women are always hunting after your memories. They have an instinct. If they sense something hidden, shut-off, they're on the hunt and they're relentless, single-minded; they are evolutionarily gifted at scanning for patterns in the past that might foretell risk in the future. I could see them pick up the scent at my first evasion and a predatory instinct take hold. But Ruby had shown no interest in my past, my memories, or my problems. For which I was truly grateful. That didn't mean I wasn't interested in hers.

As she bit my knuckle harder and closed her eyes, I asked myself, what was she getting in return from me? A tangle of fish hooks and wires, nuts and bolts, nails and screws, which, being shiny, might be mistaken for jewels, but were actually only a nasty jumble of the sharp and the dull, a disappointing lure, painful and prickly when snapped up, and made less dangerous only by the way I'd got the sharp parts twisted up in bindings.

Only six years old.

I pictured the little girl, Ruby's daughter, looking up at her mother, holding her hand, baby fat still stored for growing. Ruby's breath warmed my hand as she spoke.

I carried her to the hospital, but it was overflowing. The sick were outside on the grass and in people's yards. They gave me some pills and some water and I sat on the grass and tried to get her to swallow. I chewed up the pills and pushed them into her mouth, but she never swallowed. She took her last breaths there. I carried her back to her bed and tucked her in.

Ruby stopped crying through an act of will. She took my hand out of her mouth and gave it back to me. Looking at my fish tank she took two deep breaths, reset her shoulders, and flipped a well-worn switch inside herself. With a factual voice she told me that after her daughter died, she and her husband Francisco were done. They'd had a good marriage but grief put them on opposite sides of a river and they had no way to cross back. Her parents were dead and she had no siblings. There was nothing to keep her, so she left. She felt like she had woken in a new world—empty, wiped clean, with her eyes open. She'd started to walk south, past suburbs and industrial parks. By then there was no electricity or gas and no cars on the roads. The border was empty. She wanted to walk down every road she found. Ruby scavenged for two full turns of the seasons—berries, fruit, snails, deserted homes, begging. There were crows everywhere, so she was never alone. Occasionally she encountered dogs that had recently packed, and she learned to keep a scrap to throw them and to carry a big stick. All that time walking, not talking to anyone, she said. One day I walked into the city. A woman on the street corner was singing opera. She wasn't busking, she was just singing to people. It made me want to dance again.

I think Ruby told me all of this at this point in our relationship. I listened to her with complete attention, the way you listen to instructions for operating an automatic weapon or a chainsaw, or the way you remember saying wedding vows or watching the birth of your child—I remember everything, but not necessarily in order. The information about her floats whole cloth in my mind, nonsequentially.

I asked what kind of dance she did.

Wrong question, she said. Not what kind, but why. I'm hungry for the new. Ravenous for the new. I'm afraid we'll stop the process of destroying and tearing down too soon. We need to keep going if we're going to break through to something truly different. I push the audience to stay uncertain, unsteady, to feel strong enough to keep not knowing without filling the void. I show them how, with my body.

Ruby stopped, looked me in the eyes. That's one reason. She paused. When I perform, I keep my daughter close. Her heart beats right after mine, her hand moves with mine. I keep her close. I feel her body beside me. I know destruction is a part of life. It isn't personal. When I dance, I can pour gasoline on the world and light it up, and I can hold Molly in my arms and never, never put her in the ground.

She fell silent. Took a gulp of her whiskey. Then she asked about me; more, I felt, to change the subject than out of any desire to hear my story at that moment.

Ruby. I listened to the sound of her name in the air. I lingered on the plushness of its two syllables. Ru-by. I tilted my chair onto its hind legs. It's not that I have regrets, I said, and craned my neck violently toward the window. What I've done is beyond regret.

She tracked me closely.

Everything was legal, I said, sanctioned by authority and by society, I did nothing that everyone else did not do, but over time, over time, that has revealed itself to be so much worse than nothing.

The goldfish flashed among their plastic greenery.

And I knew better.

Tears rose, and I took a couple of seconds to shove them down. That was as far as I was dipping my toe in. She didn't pursue the subject, for which I loved her.

March 30 |

There are two main philosophical questions to human existence. Who am I? Why am I here?

I have lost interest in the first question. The answer no longer matters.

But why am I here? Even now, with the worms beckoning and my Beretta vibrating at me across the counter, I feel there's a reason, though I don't consider the feeling trustworthy.

We humans are an impossible species. Over the next few weeks when Ruby continued to show no interest in my past, despite my relief at not having to tell, I began to feel disappointed and even somewhat annoyed. I began to trawl with a baited line.

Did I wake you last night? I asked after I turned the alarm off one morning. Our bodies had drifted apart in sleep, but our hips were touching and her leg lay over mine. I turned on my side and scooped her in, my chin resting on her head, smelling the cedar and the oil from her hair.

I had a nightmare that I haven't had in years.

When she didn't ask what it was about, I showed more leg, so to speak.

I worried that you might get cold because I always wake up drenched when I have that dream.

She stretched—which also happened to break my embrace—and lifted her arms above her head and pointed her toes, flexing every muscle. I was beside a human board. She let out a big breath and rolled away, threw the covers off, and stood up.

No, I slept like a log, she answered breezily as she walked to the chair in the corner and began to get dressed. She seemed to keep her motions deliberately graceless.

I was beginning to feel like a two-year-old with a massive knot of conflicting needs and no ability to delay gratification. The only mature thing about me was the fact I could hide how much I was unravelling.

That evening I told her, I'd like to see your performance. She had just polished off a whole chicken, minus the leg and wing that I ate, a heap of mashed potatoes, and steamed curly kale with garlic and oil. My food ration for the month was depleted. Where can I buy a ticket?

She licked her fingers. You have an interest in dance?

Of course, I laughed. Clearly I've always loved dance. Season's tickets. The works.

What herbs did you use on this chicken? One of your best yet, Allen. She looked out the window. I don't want you to come.

· What if she left one day and never came back? I would never be able to find her. I mentally tested out that reality, going back to my life as it had been before her, and discovered it would no longer be bearable. I was ruined.

Break a leg, I said peevishly.

She turned on me, eyes blazing, ready to fire, and then good humour seemed to overtake her. Okay, come. I'll leave a ticket for you at the door. It's at the Meany Theatre on the old university campus. Opening night is next Wednesday at eight.

The number of dance performances I've seen I can count on one hand, if you include my mother making me watch *Cats* and *Mamma Mia!* when I was a kid and a European film I saw a couple of years ago called *Predator vs. Alien* that I thought was going to be an action thriller but which turned out to be some kind of mix of animation, choral music, and interpretive dance. A dancer began miming death from a sickness like the one that killed Jennifer, convulsing and arching, and I stood up and started yelling at the screen in rage. I was thrown out.

Ruby picked a bone up from her plate and gnawed at a shred of meat near the joint. I'm running an errand tomorrow, she said. I won't be coming over.

She was so very good at leaving no room for questions.

I needed to find out where she lived. I needed something so that if she left I could find her. When I'd asked, she said she lived in a rooming house near the theatre with a shared kitchen and bathroom. She actually called my place "cozy." No one in their right mind would call my place cozy.

I left for work at the usual time, leaving Ruby in bed with tea and cooked oats in a thermal container. On the street I texted in sick to Velma, went to the depot, and picked up a one-seater co-op car. I drove to my street and parked. The car reeked of herb. A glass jar of home-rolled butts was in the cup holder. I emptied them in the gutter. Around ten o'clock Ruby came out. She was wearing a pair of walking shoes I'd never seen before. She'd said her room was near the theatre, but when she reached Liberty Avenue, she turned away from downtown. Luckily for me, Liberty was a straight street and a main one so it was easy to follow her in spurts at a distance. She went into the Liberty Co-op depot and shortly afterward drove a vehicle out of the garage. I followed her onto the highway. We drove an extravagant fifty kilometres north, exiting just past Everett. A few minutes later she turned into the parking lot of a cemetery.

I parked on the street and followed at a distance on foot, watching her small figure walk along the driveway, then turn right and begin to thread her way through the gravestones. She disappeared from my sightline, and I guessed that she was kneeling or bending down. An hour passed. I was getting fidgety and thinking somehow she'd left without my seeing, though I couldn't imagine how, and I was deciding whether to go looking for her when she stood up and hurried out.

I walked over to where I thought she'd been and found the reason she had come. Molly Blades, May 6, 2025–February 21, 2031, beloved daughter of Ruby and Francisco. Today was February 21, 2047.

The fog was mean and low as I walked to the auditorium on the edge of the old university campus. It penetrated my clothes and my skin until even my veins and vessels were chilled. A cool pale lamp above the door lit up a sandwich chalkboard displaying the words: Dance Tonight, original choreography and performance by Ruby Blades, Sam Nygaard on the tar and guitar. A long line of people, perceptible by the jiggling beams of their Callebauts, talked and moved to keep warm. I was surprised by how many people there were. I had assumed that, since the die-off, everyone was bunkered down just trying to survive, stay warm, and hope that the worst would pass them by. But no, it seemed that people had been living all along, going to the theatre, gathering for dinners, maybe even parties. I humped to the back of the line and waited.

The majority of people were under thirty, clustered in groups of three or four, knit caps pulled down, eyes peering out, scarves wound up to their lips. About a third were my age or older, and these stood in groups of two—couples or friends. I began to sour standing there in the line. I began to feel an edge of—I'd like to say it was ambivalence—about the crowd, but contempt would be more accurate. And resentment. As a soldier, it's hard not to have some degree of contempt for high culture. None of it seems worth dying for. Or killing for.

The new names of some of the streets—Liberty Avenue for example, Liberation Street, Freedom Boulevard—also irritate me. Those words, fine words, have had their meaning sucked dry by government propaganda. They sound like products advertised in a women's magazine. We need names to wash the slate clean, names to release the citizens from carrying forward the baggage of the past, names to let us travel more lightly into the future. These people in the line with me—what were they here for? Were they searching for something new, were they looking for relief, for comfort, for reassurance? I couldn't tell what they were doing here. They seemed to be very conscious of themselves and spoke loudly, as though they were the performers looking for an audience, and that irritated me too.

The line moved forward, and I began to worry—what if I hated her performance? What if it seemed pretentious or trivial or ridiculous? I am not a good liar. She was right; I should not have come.

Ruby had left a ticket for me at the door. I chose a seat far enough back that she definitely wouldn't see my face and on the aisle so I could straighten my prosthesis. A couple of rows ahead a young man with reddish-brown curls and a pale blue-eyed face was scanning the people coming in. He looked at me and smiled. He looked familiar, but I couldn't place him. He whispered something in his friend's ear, then stood, climbed over people's legs, and came over to me. He held his head low and hunched, a bit like a boxer; he was strong across the shoulders but padded and soft in the middle.

Excuse me sir, he said. I don't mean to bother you, but you look a lot like my Uncle Allen.

Suddenly I felt afraid, unanchored. I'd spent the last seventeen years shrinking my memory to fit a territory no bigger than my apartment and my parking beat, and now, suddenly, I worried that I'd gone too far. I had no idea who this young man was. Surely I'd remember if I had more than one brother, and if that brother had fathered more than two girls. My wife was an only child.

You must be mistaken, I said. The young man returned to his seat.

The lights dimmed, the audience settled, the lights went out. A spotlight exposed Ruby in its beam, her muscles already flexed, looking out at us. Her eyes were lined with black, her lips in red, her face was white, her nose angular and prominent in the stage light. The theatre was silent except for the sound of one single vibrating note plucked rhythmically on the tar. She lifted her hand and opened her fingers, like the unfolding of a fan, then reversed the motion. She lifted both hands and unfurled them. Reversed the motion. She built on a series of simple openings and closings, each time shrinking more, building the speed and variation, whirling in a flurry of pulsing expansion and retraction until her body folded into a ball, only her back and rounded spine visible, her limbs and head tucked and curled inside. The music stopped. She stood and folded in half, limp.

The theatre filled with warm applause, and she rose, smiling, bringing us all in together to somewhere intimate, beautiful, and dangerous.

Then the stage went black. Notes sounded on a guitar this time—graceful, intricate—and a light came up on the musician, a man about forty years old, folded intimately over his instrument. I wanted to kill him. A blue light came up on Ruby who stood, head bent, waiting. She raised her head, and a slow, hypnotic melody came out of her, something about the birds are singing, but where are you, they sing their hearts out while my heart stays empty. She sang a verse in another language, I think it was Portuguese, and the volume of her voice built until it soared over the room. Watching her, my eyes felt like rivets drilled into the side of a tank. Tight, close. Every movement she made, every sound she uttered was heightened, stripped bare, exposed in a raw clarity. She created and destroyed herself over and over, pushing herself to physical and emotional extremes I found unimaginable. She became otherworldly to me. The woman on the stage was the woman who ate at my table and slept in my bed—but she inhabited two worlds, and one, the world on the stage, was unreachable to me. I was in awe. My heart ached.

The performance closed with an old blues song—Sometimes I feel like a motherless child—but she added an element—Sometimes I feel like a childless mother, and folded her arms around emptiness.

I silenced a sob in my throat but could not hold back the tears. I wiped my face on my sleeve several times. When the lights came up I was still wiping my face. The young man glanced back at me, and I nodded. His friends were leaving. He grabbed one of them by the elbow, said something, then fought the departing crowd to come to me.

My name's Griffin. I'm your brother's stepson. The last time you saw me I was, like, fourteen, so you might not recognize me.

I was astonished. I remembered really liking him. He told me he was now growing carrots. He'd studied agronomy and specialized in irrigation and soil sciences. And he played in a band. Just broke up with his girlfriend. Lived on the edge of town but it was an easy bike ride in.

He glanced up at the balcony. He said, It was like the family dropped off the face of the earth after Nan's funeral. I assumed everyone had died.

I looked away too. I wasn't sure I wanted to hear about who made it and who didn't.

How are you, Uncle Allen?

Let me give you my coordinates, I said. You haven't seen my sons by any chance?

No.

I did see Leo recently.

He looked wary, but interested. Does Leo know where my mother and sisters are?

I don't think so.

Griffin got his mobile out and I gave him my information.

Do you want to grab a drink? he asked.

Don't drink anymore. Besides, I winked, I'm with the dancer.

He grinned. No shit!

Griffin, I have to tell you. I'm a wreck. I don't have anything to offer.

He looked at me and shrugged. I miss the family. Nan, everyone, but I'm okay you know. I don't *need* anything.

I told him he'd be welcome to drop by my place any time. He pulled on his toque and bounced out of there.

I waited for Ruby on a broken chair outside the dressing room. The musician left. About a quarter of an hour later, she opened the door. Her hair was plastered to her skull except for a few wisps that had dried. She was drawn and pale and sunken under the eyes. I worried whether she would have the strength to walk in those red sandals, whether her bare legs would get too cold. I started to tell her what I thought about her performance, and she put her finger to my lips. No words.

Back at my place I wrapped a blanket around her, made her some tea, and cooked dinner. She ate automatically, her usual enormous quantity but without her usual gusto. I washed the dishes, led her to bed, took her shoes off, and lay down beside her as she slipped into a deep sleep. I wasn't tired. I stared out the window at the dark, which, over the period of half an hour, gained a thin light. Must have been from the moon and stars. The clouds must've blown away. Eventually that black turned to navy, then to ever-lightening shades of gray.

I didn't go to work. It was International Cooperation Day. I brought her tea, then let her fall back asleep with her head on my shoulder. I guess my heartbeat rocked her dreams. I was alive again, and she was responsible.

I've been writing for three weeks now and my ambush is almost laid. Writing about Ruby has distracted me from my torment, but I'm getting tired. Velma gives me the hairy eyeball when I come into work and sniffs the air to show me she smells the booze. Larry avoids looking at me. I woke this morning filled with dread and sorrow, the fragments still with me from a dream about Ruby being locked in some kind of hut with giant chicken legs and me fighting through worms to try and unlock the door. The hut took off over the hills, and I called in anguish as she vanished. The tentacles of that anguish reach through to waking reality. I must pounce soon or I won't make it.

Ruby and I had a couple of blissful weeks after I saw her performance. She came over every night to eat and sleep. I never went to her place.

Then I mentioned the boys. It was a Sunday, and we'd gone back to bed after eating a big breakfast. I think the happiness and warmth with her was making me unguarded, and I let the feeling of missing them come out.

You have sons! And you don't try to find them? What kind of man are you? You work at this job, day in, day out, while your children are in the world without you?

They're grown men, Ruby.

Children grow up. That's the point.

I did my duty by them.

Wow.

She leapt out of bed, grabbed my T-shirt, put it on, and went and stood by the window. She looked up at the sky with her arms wrapped tight around herself and gnawed the side of her finger.

You know. If I had my daughter ...

I was a drowning man. Everything had been going along swimmingly and suddenly I was drowning. *Hey, I'm drowning here!* I wanted to yell to someone on the shore.

I am the kind of man whose sons are better off without him, I said.

She looked up higher at the sky and pressed herself against the window as though every part of her wanted to leave this room.

How to explain such a statement? I'd have to tell her my story. I'm a soldier—we're wired to risk our lives. I could tell her the memories that bring the knives out and slice through my mind like a sushi chef. I ran through the risk/reward calculations. Then something in me bolted.

Besides, I said, it's not really any of your business.

A look of disgust came into her eyes. She got dressed and left.

I was so restless I had to leave my apartment. I exhausted myself walking all over the city. Over the next few days my stump blistered badly from constant friction with my prosthesis and I worried no amount of cream would prevent callusing.

The worms are out in full regalia. They're wearing party hats of green and pink and yellow, tossing confetti, and doing the can-can.

Allen! We knew you'd come!

They take my arm to lead me down the hall where the party is. I am dazed and numb. I don't know if I'm coming or going. I have no will and no fear. But as I'm being ushered by joyous threadlike arm after arm, I feel they are rushing me. I feel, behind their gaiety, they want to get me into the party before I change my mind. I try to come to a stop, to dig in my heel, but the force of all those cilia-like arms pushing me toward the entrance and the slight imbalance of my one leg mean I can only slow my pace.

Allen? They raise their eyebrows and look at me with disapproving sadness and disappointment. What's wrong, Allen? This party's for you. We've gone to so much trouble. Don't you like it?

I catch a glimpse of a steel coffin and a posse of worms on top trying to pry it open with a crowbar.

I turn the top half of my body to face the direction in which I came and start to fight my way back, keeping my arms close and my head down like a quarterback. They ramp up the gaiety, laughing and dancing and hugging each other, and I have to knock a few down (they offer a soft, springy resistance) to get back through the portal.

A week passed and Ruby stayed away. I couldn't bear being home, but walking long distances was no longer an option because the callused skin on my stump cracked, so I'd go down by Duwamish Waterway and sit on a bench.

Nobody lingers outside anymore. The wind, the rain, the sun, the clouds, they all make us uneasy. I don't know why anyone bothered to make the bench. No one will ever sit there.

I sat and looked across the waterway, ten times wider than in the old days. New leaves were a yellow-green blur against bark that glowed pink with new sap. Six meters in front of me the masts of sunken yachts from the old marina stuck out of the water at odd angles. The long evening progressed and fog slunk in, hugging the shoreline at first, then gradually spreading out over the water.

Ten women walking down a path on my right interrupted my solitude. They pulled ropes attached to a trailer carrying a dragon boat. Silently, they eased the contraption down to the water's edge and set the boat in the water. The drummer set up her drum and took her perch, the sweep positioned herself at the stern, and the rest got in and pushed off onto the grey-green water, rowing slowly backward, the sweep calling out instructions to avoid shallow-water obstacles. They disappeared in the fog. The last thing I saw was the boat's green dragon head with its red tongue lolling out between white teeth. Then I heard the drum. I assumed they'd reached deeper water.

In some ways the world is more beautiful than it was before.

On the eighth evening what I had to do came clear. I humped and stumped over to the library.

My sons. I believe they are better off without me. When Jennifer gave birth to them, I'd felt ferocious—I would fight for them, I would kill for them, I would die for them—but when I came back from my last tour of duty the question had been: could I live for them? I'd been trying to protect them by staying distant, but now, with Ruby opening me up, maybe I did have something to offer them.

The library chair was a hard wooden one at a long wooden table. I rested my head on my hands on the table. Already my inner cats were starting to yowl and hiss. Their claws were starting to penetrate the bag and scratch at my intestines and the membrane around my heart. The tight band I'd forged around my life to keep it purified of importance had been weakened by Ruby, and my life was expanding like a down sleeping bag being pulled out of a stuffbag. But with the softening of the heart came harder things that poked their noses out and I could feel aggression concentrating in their snouts and honing in. I was going to have to act quickly.

The web grid has expanded again gradually since the die-off, though it's still nowhere near what it was before. Only people in cities have mobiles and only fifty percent at that. With the latest web expansion, a missing persons site has at last been created. Velma found her sister and a childhood girlfriend through it. Larry found his father. The librarian gave me the site address and I set up an account. Three messages popped up for an Allen Levy Quincy, last residing in Cascadia. My heart filled with doom. I opened the mailbox. Old messages from Leo, Griffin, and a cousin on my father's side from Utah, now the Administrative Department of the Great Plains. I posted my boys' names, Luke Quincy (Leapin' Luke) and Sam Quincy (Smokin' Sam or Smoke), and filled in the date last seen, location last seen, relationship, and my coordinates.

I did it for Ruby. But I also hoped it would be good for all of us. They were almost grown men when they left. They'd be able to decide for themselves.

I could have looked through the obituaries but could not bear the thought of finding their names there.

When I found Ruby again I didn't want to appear as desperate as I was, but deception has never been my strong point. My only strategy therefore was to be direct and honest. I went over to the university and bought a ticket for her performance. It was closing night, which gave me a chill. I'd almost lost her. After the performance I waited outside her dressing room. When she opened the door, I pulled off my toque and began to sing a Nirvana song my first babysitter introduced me to, "Come as You Are." I leaned in close and sang in a whisper, starting with the instrumental part.

I stopped at the song's bridge, thinking that swearing you don't have a gun wouldn't hit the emotional note I was aiming for. I told her I had registered my sons on the missing persons website. I told her I missed her. And then I said, I have something to tell you, something I've never told anyone, something it might destroy me to tell. I think it's the only way forward. She cocked her head and raised an eyebrow.

I was hurtling into space strapped to a bucket seat. We got to my apartment and I led her to bed and undressed her, my heart exploding. We made love twice and I let out a holler, an indefinable sound. She laughed. I fed her. She fell asleep and I dozed.

I woke up a couple of hours before sunrise. I put on my leg and my bathrobe and stole quietly out to the kitchen. I put my overcoat on over my bathrobe to keep warm, poured some cold tea, and sat in my chair looking out the window at the blackness. I began to make out the shapes of clouds moving across the sky, then the blooms of a magnolia across the street started to glow through their net. A cyclist floated by, the beam of his Callebaut projecting a thin line of light from the handlebars.

In a way, everything in my life before now seemed to have had the purpose of bringing me to this moment with the intention of speaking. And having arrived at this moment, there was no way back. My old strategy was in ruins. Ruby, with her prodigious appetite and big stride, had woken me up and going back to sleep was not an option. Everything seemed volatile and impermanent.

I thought: maybe I have another ten years to live, maybe twenty. I want her in them if possible. I thought: time could be a large airy room we inhabit together. She would never abide being cornered and we both had wounds that wouldn't heal, wounds that required privacy, yet I thought in a big enough space we could love each other.

Speaking now was the only way forward yet the risks were chittering and hissing and fluttering in the air around me.

I thought about the smallest particle of matter, the Higgs boson that Ruby had mentioned, changing from the force of being looked at.

Eventually a guttural, exhaling growl of pleasure, the kind people make when they stretch, came from my bedroom. I put the kettle on and brought my beloved a hot cup of tea. She had one arm above her head and held that hand with the other and pulled, stretching the side of her body. I put the tea on the floor beside the bed, sat down, and rested a hand on her leg, which was under the covers.

From my seat in the dark theatre I had seen a crowd pass through her: orphan, refugee, seductress, gatherer, pregnant mother, madwoman, oracle, huntress. She was a childless mother, a gypsy, and an artist who knew the world, yet no one knew her. I wanted to be the man who knew her. I felt the pulse in her leg under my hand. I felt her, but I did not know her, not in the way I'd known Jennifer. In the old days I would never have loved Ruby; she would have been too unfamiliar, too unpredictable.

She sipped her tea and looked at me. It felt like we were in a space capsule.

Sitting on my bed with my hand on her leg I believed it could work. I could tell her and we would live happily ever after, safe on the platform of my bed, two bodies making love and bringing home food and news until we grew old and died. The best ending a human can hope for.

I lay down beside her and started to talk at the ceiling. I moved into hyper-clarity, tracing the tiny valleys and peaks of the stucco's texture. I can summon the exact shade of grey made by the light coming through my window on the dark side of each knobble of plaster.

She lay on her side looking at me, her hands tucked under her face, satisfied, relaxed, full. *That* was a miracle. I jumped off the cliff and began.

Two years before the die-off peaked, my battalion was deployed to a camp in the desert to guard the border wall between Mexico and the North. The main conflict, you'll remember, was in the Arctic Circle, keeping the Russians and Norwegians out, but we were sent south. The Mexicans were blowing holes in the wall because they desperately needed water. When we arrived the breaches had been filled with barbed-wire coils and at night the place was lit up like a movie set. We heard stuff like this was going on along the length of the entire wall. On the second night the wind began to blow. Even with masks on, we breathed in the dust. It was like being on Mars. I didn't think anything could survive out there in the dark without masks, without water.

Tumbleweeds would get caught in the wire coils, then the wind would shift and the weeds would be blown back into the dark or come straight at us and make us jump. One night, sometime before dawn, three RPGs went off and a couple of our guys got hit by fragmentation. The flash from the launcher showed as a brief glow on the other side of the wall but in all that dust you couldn't see smoke trails to pinpoint the origin. The tumbleweeds started really freaking everyone out. You'd be peering into the brown haze lit by the spotlights and this round ball would catapult out of nowhere into your face. I put my weapon down and tried to karate chop the suckers before they touched me. I remember the feel of dried sticks roiling off the side of my hand and some of the twigs blowing into my face. And I remember the dust. And the brown haze. And the dust from the new holes in the wall that we couldn't see until we got lights on them, but sensed as a darker patch in the haze.

Ruby rolled onto her back and joined me staring at the ceiling. I took a few shallow breaths and continued.

By the time we shipped out three months later to go back home we were just lucky there was enough fuel for the buses.

We had to carry all the fuel for the journey back with us. As we entered the base my sons must've heard the buses because they came racing into the clearing area. They flew at me when I stepped out of the door. I placed my hand on their shaggy heads and looked for Jennifer.

The heat of their skulls radiated through their damp hair and I was filled with revulsion. For three months all I'd wanted was to return home to them and now I jerked my hand away and covered my behaviour by getting the boys to look for my bag and challenging them to carry it all the way home.

As I spoke I was hyper-aware of Ruby's breathing. We weren't touching. Out of the blue a desire for a drink hit me hard and I had to stop talking and wait for it to pass. Ruby's breathing was as steady as a metronome.

The boys took turns carrying my bag. Sam dragged it more than carried it back to the house. I don't know why Jennifer didn't come out to the buses. She must've known it was our battalion. My parents, who'd moved back onto the base when the troubles started, hurried over. Jennifer stood holding the door open for the boys to drag my bag in, and my parents hovered behind her. My mom didn't look good. She was thin and pale and hunched over.

I got to the foot of the steps and hesitated. I didn't want to pass over the doorsill. I looked down at the ground. I noticed the blades of grass, some green, some yellow, and clover and buttercups. A line of ants beside the path was running bits of leaf. I noticed them meet head on and sort out their impulses, go left or go right, two choices, a binary decision. I started to cry. Jennifer ran down the stairs to hug me and I held up my arm—No—my first word back.

I did eventually walk into the house. No one wanted to upset me, so they hung back, waiting for a sign. I went to the bathroom and locked the door. They must've heard the weird gasping sounds I made trying to sob silently. After a while, my dad came to the door and spoke. I wasn't sobbing out of grief. It was just a way to let off pressure. I wasn't feeling anything except that I didn't want them to know how numb I was. I opened the bathroom door and announced, I'm going to the den to play some video games.

I started drinking heavily and playing on-line games all day. The army shrink told my family that it was post-traumatic stress disorder. It was, but it was also more than that. My whole understanding of the world had changed. My father took me out for a beer. I drank four to his one. Five to his one. Son, he said. Tell me what happened. I'm ashamed to say that I went on the attack. I belittled his service. I belittled him for never having killed.

Ruby clasped her hands below her breasts above the blankets. She lay like a painting of drowned Ophelia—hair spread out—very pale, as people in excellent physical condition sometimes are after extreme exertion. I couldn't tell for sure if she was listening.

My father reached across the table and grasped my forearm in his strong, dry hand. My leg was going like a pneumatic drill. I was trembling and sweating and glancing wildly all over the place. I searched his face with the faint hope that he might have something to offer, some wisdom or knowledge, but there was nothing. All I saw was helplessness and love. He loved me. He really loved me.

I told him I had to go and downed my glass and fled before I hurt him any more. It was the last time I saw him healthy. He died two weeks later of the influenza.

I paused in my telling just as I've paused now, in my writing. Breathed. Breathed in. Then jumped headlong.

On our second night the Mexicans blew another hole in the wall. Amid the swirling smoke and dust lit up by our floodlights a man walked out of the darkness and stood in the new breach. He was covered in dust and his face was shadowed by a hat, a cloth hat with a wide soft brim, like a gardener's hat. We couldn't see his face but we felt him looking at us. No one moved. We waited. Then he moved his hand very slightly and people began to stream out of the darkness behind him and walk past him through the new hole.

They were silent. In all that wind and dust, with all the orders being shouted and guys yelling, you could hear that they were silent. Our orders were to shoot anyone breaching the wall. The floodlights exposed them: women, children, old people, sons, daughters—expressionless, focused only on getting through and disappearing into the darkness on our side. When we saw it was civilians I ordered my company to fire warning shots, but the people didn't even slow down. I was getting orders on my headset to stop the motherfuckers and I was yelling back that it was kids and women and old people. *Stop them, I don't care how, but stop them. No one crosses.* I called out a warning in English and again in Spanish but they didn't even look up. I shouted an order to my men to use non-lethal force. Our first shots were to legs and feet, and a whimper went through the crowd, but people just lifted the wounded under their arms and carried them forward. Someone must have told them not to run, not to panic, not to scream, that their only hope was to just keep walking forward. Other units were firing at other breaches along the wall and we heard a C6 and an FN Mag open fire. I prayed for the crowd to turn back. I shut my eyes and pleaded with the universe to turn them back, but of course it didn't. They needed a drink of water. They needed food. They poured through, heading for darkness while the man with the hat stood looking at us.

The major on the other end of my headset demanded to know what was wrong. *Stop them, or I'll stop you.*

I wish I could tell you I said, Go ahead, stop me.

I flipped the switch. I wish I could say it was my training that kicked in, but it wasn't. I felt rage. Rage that I was in that position, and rage that my men were. There was anguish and pain and horror, but on top of that, there was rage, and it coalesced into one thought—make this stop, shut this down. End it. We took out the man with the hat first. All night they kept coming, as if they thought we might run out of bullets. They had to climb over bodies to keep coming. When I say bodies, you think dead bodies, but many of our shots were not fatal. Our earlier kindness in shooting to injure we soon regretted. During a pause in the exodus, as we stood with our guns pointing toward the heap of bodies, we heard moaning and crying and muffled wailing and groaning. Children crying Mama, Mama, Papa, and women, mothers calling Eduardo, Anna, Maria, Carlos. Men calling for their wives, their children, sisters and brothers, friends. No one crying for themselves.

It was like a massive birthing gone wrong. Bodies covered with sweat and blood and tears, hair glued to heads like a newborn's, flesh blue and white, glistening and streaked with darker blood.

I asked for permission to terminate the wounded. The major was gentle with me now: We don't know how bad this thing is going to get. I know it's hard, Quincy, but you need to save bullets for the ones coming over.

I thought of going to take a piss and then just keeping on walking, but unless I took my men with me, I wasn't leaving.

My soul—and the souls of many of my men—leached out that night. I could feel it coming out of me; there was a sensation to it, like blood leaking from the heart, electricity from the brain. Damage that you know is permanent as it is being inflicted.

The morning after, it rained. My lieutenant put his 9mm in his mouth and pulled the trigger. I remember him bending over the muzzle of his lowered weapon and opening his mouth and I thought, Odd time for a sexual joke.

All those people wanted was a simple drink of water, and here it came, for free. I think we would have killed God, or whoever it was that set the world up this way, right then. The rainwater ran off the bodies, washing their blood away. I looked down at my friend, in chunks from the neck up. Anyone walking through the hole that morning I let pass. There weren't many. An American commander drove up, saw what was going on, and said something like, If you let them in, Americans are going to die. They would shoot us if the situation were reversed, in a heartbeat. Are you fucking soldiers or aren't you? I almost shot him just to shut him up.

We stayed there for another three months.

Some men started to take the women aside first. The kids would go nuts, screaming for their mothers.

For the acts I committed at that time I was given the nickname Mercy.

I could not continue speaking for a while.

Then I said, I will never kill again.

Tears started in my eyes. I stopped them.

Horror is not surprising, I said. Not at all. It's surprisingly familiar. An old friend on the street who you recognize even at a distance. It's not unimaginable at all. People who say it is are lying.

I stopped speaking. The sides of the rabbit hole were hurtling by at speed as I sank into the earth. Ruby wasn't reaching out a hand. I could not speak in that instant, yet had Ruby said something it would have been a lifeline. Eventually, desperation made me babble on.

I have subsisted, not dying and not living, until I met you. And you have taken me somewhere as close to free as I am ever going to be. Are you wondering if I'm sane? What makes me sane is that I see you and I want you; nothing else in this world makes sense. I see you and blood goes to my penis, cause and effect. That's a kind of sanity.

I became a soldier, I laughed bitterly, to end killing.

I fell silent.

Two sisters walk hand-in-hand down the road, their backs turned to me, whispering secrets in each other's ears: Murder and Suicide.

Murder: the coward's form of suicide.

Suicide: the coward's form of murder.

I came to this afternoon in my armchair, two empties by my feet, and the worms making their entrance from the out-side corner of my eyes, using my lids as their stage curtain. Mardi Gras hadn't let up one bit. Twelve worms in party hats, whirling noisemakers and tossing confetti, danced the Macarena toward the bridge of my nose and assembled on my cheekbone to do the hip grind part right in front of my eyeballs. I was mesmerized, to say the least. I wanted to join their party and leave myself behind forever.

The spokesworm climbed up to the bridge of my nose and lifted his arms for silence. The others moved back to listen. I was cross-eyed watching him.

> *David he wrote words of sin*
> *Goliath came and clocked him*
> *David tried to write some more*
> *Goliath feigned a little snore*
> *Then up and got 'im in a headlock*
> *Mussing up poor David's dreadlocks*
> *Let my memories go, D cried*
> *Golly's laughter was rather snide*
> *Hey there Moses of the mind*
> *It's your meat I'm going to grind*
> *Golly said, you'll never win, see?*
> *Which made Allen Quincy*
> *Even more wincy!*

At this last line all the worms broke out dancing and singing again, waving their arms in the air and blowing whistles. Those closest to my left eyelid began to exit the stage by ducking under and the others followed. C'mon, Quincy, what you got to lose? asked the spokesworm.

As I was considering my answer to this question, I heard pounding. The noise persists and I am thinking maybe it exists outside my head. Maybe someone is pounding on the door.

Allen! Allen! I know you're in there, bro. Open up. I got a plan I want to tell you about.

I lay my pencil down. My mother's journal is puffy now, the pages crinkled from the force of the pencil lead pressing down on the paper. He can't be certain I'm here.

C'mon, Allen. Hear me out, he thumps again. It's the last thing I'll ask of you before I die. One last thing. Open the door.

I see now that a writer is a kind of tactician with a limited array of materiel. One must consider how to deploy one's weapons and plan the order, timing, and pacing: attack, ambush, invade, surrender. I believe I have failed. My strategy has failed.

Leo thumps on the door again, a frustrated whack. C'mon, ya bastard, open up! It's a good plan. You owe me a hearing at least. Then, in a wheedling voice, I heard your boys are there. We gotta go find them.

I leap up and pull the door open. Leo's crouching by the keyhole. He looks up at me.

My boys! How have you heard from them? Do you have their coordinates?

No, no, I don't.

You're lying. You don't know anything.

I heard. I heard from a guy.

I am going to close the door now. Don't bother me again. I close the door.

C'mon, bro. What you got to lose?

I feel like I pulled the pin on a grenade but I'm failing to throw it.

I go to pour a drink. One of the goldfish floats up to the surface. Its beautiful, translucent fins, white and long, look like the thing at the end of a wedding dress.

My story becomes a betrayal in the writing down of it. It's a sordid little deal: in exchange for exposing the suffering and death of other people to any Tom, Dick, or Harry who might happen to read my words, I, their murderer, get my life back.

No.

Not doing it.

Grandparents, godparents, aunts, uncles, or cousins: I could whisper the description of the victim's last minutes to them, but not to a stranger who never loved them. (That word, "victim," how I loathe it. The people trying to cross the border were people, not a subset, "victims." They should not be defined by the genocide, defined by an act they had nothing to do with. Only we, the murderers, the genociders, should be defined.) I don't even know if this will be read, or if you, my theoretical reader, a stranger, will indulge in the *schadenfreude* that you, at least, are still alive, or worse, if you'll get a manic jolt, a whiff of omnipotence, the pleasure of power over others ignited in you, but I must assume the possibility because you, my reader, if you exist, will also be human.

Writing is pornographic. It is like forcing prisoners to perform a striptease of their suffering in front of an anonymous crowd—their exposure a final, sadistic, posthumous indignity.

I grasp my head between my hands and squeeze.

They're dead, I whisper. What expense to them if I pinch their pockets? Their souls, already long released, what does it matter to them if I tell their story to save *my* soul?

I get up to pour myself another depth charge. My hand is shaking. I've lost count, but I just drained another bottle of R & R that, mere hours ago, was full. Two empties stand beside it. There's still one more full bottle waiting under the kitchen sink. I haven't been outside in three days. I haven't returned Velma's text messages. I'm not sure I'll ever go back to work. I haven't slept and I'm down to a jar of pickles and a box of stale crackers.

While I'm shoving crackers in my mouth Leo comes back. I want to strangle him. He bangs on my door and calls my name, then I hear the fabric of his clothes rub the door as he slumps to the floor. He's breathing heavily. While I'm wondering if he's passed out and whether I can tiptoe back to the table, another set of footsteps comes up the stairs. I cringe and crouch into a ball.

Who the fuck are you? Leo slurs.

Is this the apartment of Allen Quincy?

Who wansa know?

I'm Mr Quincy's nephew.

Well I'm Mr Quincy's only brother and I don't have sons, so that's gotta make you my stepson.

Silence.

Leo?

No shit.

Uncle Allen wasn't sure he'd see you again.

So sudge luck.

Silence.

You wanna come to Nirvana?

The cabin?

A grunt.

He's not here. Take me downstairs. Grabba bite.

I bring my drink back to the table, glad they're gone.

When I told Ruby about the genocide on the border, the words were warm from my breath, but when I wrote them down they turned hard and armoured, and this fills me with disgust. Of course writing doesn't destroy memory, I've known that since just after I started, yet it does alter memory and it does destroy living memory. I thought that might be enough. Who can shoot the written word? Who can punish it or kill it? Does it die from lack of oxygen? From a broken heart? From shame? Can it lose its soul? But writing also turns private memory out onto the street like an underage runaway and makes me feel like both a pimp and a john, as well as a murderer.

My plan has failed. I'll never be cured.

Instead I'll keep guard over the only thing left to my dead: their place in my memory. I'll keep them nestled in the warmth of the pinky–grey, plushy folds of my brain, singing their requiem with electric pings leaping from neuron to neuron, spreading out in myriad branches behind the armour of my skull, their existence only as immortal as I am, tender and private, for as long as we both shall live. I will heave my shoulder to the door and use my mind as a weapon to protect them from oblivion.

I have arrived at the exact opposite result of what I intended, a turn of events that, I imagine, is not unfamiliar to writers. I'm so tired. I'll pour one more R & R and slip into the black velvet arms of sleep.

I talked to Ruby well into the afternoon that day as the light brightened then waned. I emptied my memory onto her, obscenely, and she lay there and took it. Two people alone in a room.

I don't know what I expected. I was compelled to speak, regardless of the result, there was no other way out, but I suppose what I hoped was that the universe, like some kind of divine escort service, had sent Ruby to bring me happiness. All the sex of the previous six weeks—I had mistaken the experience for rebirth, but rebirth doesn't happen from the outside.

When I stopped speaking she made no comment. It was around four in the afternoon. We stared at the ceiling for a while, side by side.

I'm hungry, she said, and that was proven by an outrageous growl from her belly.

I had laid my intestines out for her to see and now I had the humiliating task of looping them up again and trying to tuck them back in, in front of her. It was going to take some time and the smell wouldn't be the best. Meanwhile, she had shown me nothing.

I dragged myself into the kitchen, to get away from her, to hide the horror that was Allen Quincy. I made her dinner. Her appetite, which had been such a delight at first, such a surprise and a joy, had become oppressive.

What did I cook? I took out some potatoes, kidney beans, a can of tomatoes. I made her a mash. It took an hour in the pressure cooker. She stayed in my bedroom, for which I was grateful. When it was cooked I added salt. I called her and managed to tuck in the last loop of guts before she came into the room and sat down. I slopped the mush into the bowl in front of her. Not my most appetizing looking meal.

She looked at it. She picked up her spoon and leaned over her bowl, my bowl, and spoke. I'm fighting my own battle Quincy. I don't have the strength to fight yours. She turned her head and glanced quickly at me. There were tears in her eyes. She looked back down at the slop I'd dished out. Whatever you want from me? What do you want? Whatever you want, her voice rose, you've opened a door here. She looked around, like a cornered animal. She was getting ready to bolt. You've opened a door here, she repeated.

I don't want you to carry anything, I said.

What did you imagine would happen? What could you have imagined?

I couldn't speak.

She stopped looking around. She took a bite of her food, chewed rapidly. Eyes fixed on her plate, she said, Either you want sympathy Quincy, or you want sex. I'm not giving you both.

I had no words.

She took another bite, chewed quickly. Her shoulders floated down from a hunched position and she reset them in her dancer's posture. She lifted her head, ready for an audience.

I'm not here—on this earth, Quincy, she pointed at the floor, to look after you. My milk days, she lifted one of her breasts the way a nursing mother does to offer the nipple to a baby, are over.

A black rage exploded through me. I grabbed her wrist and squeezed it until she dropped the spoon.

I am not here—on this earth, I said between clenched teeth, to feed you. And at this particular instant I want neither sympathy nor sex, so maybe you should leave.

My heart was breaking. I looked wildly around the room for help, at the corner of sky I could see out of my window from the kitchen. It was raining hard.

A second passed. She leapt to her feet, twisted under my arm, and broke my grasp. She backed away in a crouch, arms out, panther-like, moving side-to-side, back and forth, in a state of readiness to attack. She must have known that Brazilian martial art, Capoeira. I put my hand up and dropped my head, signalling no further attack.

She backed up to the coat hook, got her coat, and put it on. She took rain boots out of her bag and a pair of socks and perched on the arm of my easy chair to pull them on. She came over, grabbed my shoulders, dug her nails into the backs of my arms, and kissed me hard, hard enough to split my lip against my teeth.

I'd risked it all for a chance to keep her. I'd had no choice. I was in a boxed canyon.

She looked at me. I was disconcerted because there was blood on her teeth from my lip. She looked at me for a long time and went out the door.

I am still trying to comprehend that look. It wasn't goodbye. It wasn't despair. It wasn't hatred. There was rage, fiery rage, an intent to destroy, and maybe the merest flicker of curiosity.

The cupboard's empty, the fridge is empty, the bottles are empty, my journal is almost full. I put my pencil down and stare at the wall. I hear a noise, a hesitant throat clearing, from near the window. The last hue of slate-grey sky darkens and wind gusts against the windowpane.

The spokesworm steps out from behind the curtain into a pool of white light. He is wearing a top hat and tails and carrying a cane with a silver top. He holds a cordless mike and gazes out into space as though over the heads of an anonymous crowd. He looks down at his feet at the end of his short threadlike legs, as though waiting for the crowd to finish their applause and get out their last coughs and whispers, then he looks up, directly at me, and starts to sing the old 1970s classic "Send in the Clowns."

As he begins, "Isn't it rich …," a chorus of worms dressed as clowns shuffles into position in a pool of light floating just behind his right shoulder. They are wearing red, orange, yellow, and rainbow wigs, floppy hats with daisies in them, big red noses, big shoes, and loose onesies with pompom buttons. Some are happy, with big smiles painted over their mouths, and others are sad, with a teardrop painted on their cheeks. Once they are all assembled and in position—a process that involves quite a bit of jostling, friends trying to stand together, showboats striving for the centre of the spotlight—they stare soulfully straight ahead.

The song has a melancholy, world-weary, ironic tone and the spokesworm sings with all the rich smoothness and shabby grace it demands. As the lyrics contrast one of the lovers' frenetic, constant motions with the other's complete paralysis, lights come up softly on a raised platform floating behind and to the right of the chorus with a steel coffin on a viewing stand. Two worms are frantically trying to pry the lid open with crowbars.

The spokesworm looks meaningfully at me and croons the refrain, but instead of "clowns" he sings "worms"—send in the worms—which gives the song a whole new twist. He goes on to describe how one of the lovers finally decided to stop philandering and make a commitment only to find that the object of their love was no longer there, they'd moved on.

Here the clown-worms leave their pool of light and queue up by the coffin, having pried the lid open, and slowly begin to shuffle past, looking inside with exaggerated sadness. As the spokesworm sings that no one is there, the worms tilt the coffin toward me so I can see it's empty, and I know that I was the one who was supposed to be inside.

The spokesworm continues the song's wry lament about poor timing and missed connections, his voice like warm clear water gliding over smooth rocks, and the clown-worms commence a series of tumbling somersaults and handsprings in and out of the empty coffin like a troupe of gymnasts, reverting to their baseline carnival exuberance. The spokesworm looks down at his wristwatch as though seeking an answer there, but finding none, reprises the chorus, "send in the worms." The spotlight on the clown-worms fades to black.

The spokesworm stands alone, still brightly illuminated, and looks over at me with wistful hopefulness, then he shrugs and walks off the stage whispering, Maybe next year.

I woke up this morning with my pillow damp from tears and the image of Ruby looking at me, crouching and swaying back and forth, back and forth. Unusually, the sun is shining, which means everyone will be indoors. If I can get myself out before the cloud returns, I can have the world to myself.

But first, this final entry. I've made my tea—oh, it tastes good. The last few nights I've been Sinbad the Sailor with my dead clamped on my shoulders ready to cut off my air lest I forget them. Today something has lifted.

I dropped the spoon with the sugar I was about to put in my tea. My hand isn't exactly steady this morning. As I wiped the white grains of sugar into a pile and enfolded it in the cold damp cloth, something red caught my eye from under the armchair. I crawled over, lowered my cheek to the floor, and fished out a red sandal. It must've fallen out of her bag when she was getting her raingear out.

Her animal face looked at me, fight or flight, focused on flight but fight was right there. Her eyes weren't connecting with me. I remembered her squeezing my arm at the flea market, letting me know she understood how things were with her, strong and weak, but she was helpless to change them.

I held her shoe in both my hands and rubbed its worn leather with my thumbs. I know how to find her. I have found my One Pure Thing, and when I find her, I will opt out.

Someone's pounding on my door, making it hard to concentrate on writing. Brother Leo's hand reaching out to me. I am neither alive nor dead, drunk nor sober, neither dreaming nor fully awake. It's a race to write these last words before his pounding breaks the catch. He is not reaching out because he wants to save me. He is reaching out because he wants something from me.

Salvation comes in many forms.

JOURNAL
TWO

I opened my eyes. I couldn't distinguish the morning mist from the fog. I was alert, which made me guess something external to myself had woken me. I scanned for scent, searched for a visual.

My cheek was out of the tent on the ground. The forest floor smelled of late-winter rot, not punky, but a fresh, loamy smell. The dead leaves and needles were brown and damp, darker where they had already begun turning to earth, yet the humus on the surface seemed red, a dark, brick red, aggressively absorbing the growing white light of day through the mist until it was almost fluorescent.

The coldest time of day is just after the sun rises, when a biting draft comes up. This morning was no different. I was frozen.

I listened for a repetition òf the sound that might have woken me. I let my breath out very slowly. I did not yet dare feel for the knife I'd left beside me when I went to sleep.

I am alone and badly wounded.

I listened, but all I heard was my heart straining to push large volumes of blood to my muscles in preparation for battle. All I heard was the drip, drip of moisture that had coalesced in drops too heavy to cling to leaves or needles, plinking down in the forest. What I heard was nothing from the birds. Two knives would have been better, one for each hand. I cursed myself for not bringing the Beretta.

A new leaf on a salmonberry bobbed on its stem. I heard a swish, like a short out-breath or the back suck of a small wave on a pebble beach, and knew that she'd left. She'd been watching.

I lifted my head from the ground and my hand found the knife's handle. I sniffed. The mist smelled like grass before it's cut, or a trout still dripping from the river.

I don't want to give her another chance to pierce my skin.

The pain is just beginning to recede from my mind and adhere to the actual wounds. The cells on the edges are knitting together and soon they'll get itchy.

This is how I woke this morning, which is to say marginally better than yesterday.

I'm foggy about Griffin and Leo. They built a windbreak around the tent, leaving only the entrance exposed. Griffin cleaned my wounds and Leo tacked my scalp back on. They left yesterday. I think. One to paddle, one to fish. They wanted to supplement our food supplies.

I have enough wood to keep a fire burning for several days, boiled water to drink and to clean my wounds, and a small bag of salt.

My scalp is re-grafting though the tissue has shrunk and left a gap about a centimetre wide where new scar tissue is growing. The hair on the injured part of my scalp, the whole top, is coming out in tufts, and part of my upper lip is gone. Under my right eye, wounds, either from teeth or claws, I can't remember, are deep. I'll be a striking piece of work when this is done. Ruby will get a thrill, if I am ever lucky enough to see her again.

It was like getting hit with a bag of sand. The impact threw me forward onto the ground. Wildly I reached back—I had no idea at what—and got a handful of fur. She got me at the hairline, ripped my scalp back, got a new grip on my skull, dug her claws into my shoulder. My pack protected my neck.

Griffin heard something and turned back, came around the trees, and saw us. He yelled for Leo. The cougar looked up, unafraid. Leo dropped his pack and started to look for a big stick or rock. The cougar twisted her jaw, ripping deeper. I groaned. Griffin started talking to me. He took his pack off and held it in front of him and walked toward us, hoping to get her to back off.

Her breath smelled like dried spit and oil. I didn't move because I didn't want her teeth or claws to go deeper. Griffin kept talking to me, keeping her attention. She growled in a low rumble. He said her tail swished back and forth on the ground like she wanted to play. He thought it was only a question of size that made him less afraid, because he was almost twice as big.

She got a better grip on my head and dragged me a couple of feet sideways toward a steep downward slope. Griffin yelled, Leave him! and moved to cut her off. She shook her head and I yelled out in pain and reached back desperately, trying to find her eyes, her throat.

Griffin yelled for Leo again and unclipped a frying pan from his backpack. I'm going to hit her with a frying pan, Uncle Allen. When I do, fight back as hard as you can. We can take her together. She's not that big.

He lunged forward, and she pulled me further toward the slope. He whacked her with the pan on the head, though not solidly. I felt the vibration of the blow through her teeth into my skull. She snarled, increased the pressure of her jaw. He hit her again, a solid blow, and she let go, backed up, low to the ground, ready to spring at him. I got to my feet, blinded by blood. Leo came out of the forest with a big branch in one hand and a rock in the other. She glanced at Leo, turned tail, and disappeared.

Holy shit! Leo said, memorably.

If Leo and Griffin don't come back, if my wounds get infected, if the cougar returns, I want there to be more than a few bones and some rusty tent poles to tell what happened to me. I am keeping a record for as long as I can.

It's more than that. During the month I prepared for this journey I missed writing. It had become a habit, like a daily conversation, a practice. It made me feel witnessed the way, I imagine, that someone who believes in God feels witnessed. You, my future reader, have become my witness, my companion. I may not be a writer, but I have become someone who writes.

I've also started reading my other journal. There's nothing else to do. I've thrown another log on the fire, and I'm shivering in my sleeping bag. I can only write and read in short spurts before my head starts to hurt.

The cougar was beautiful. Griffin told me. I never saw her but I remember the weight and smell of her. Somewhere in the struggle I noticed that her teats were hard as fingernails and damp with milk. I'm weak but oddly energized. I feel chosen. I am giddy when not asleep.

I'm almost out of water. Tomorrow I'll have to get more. Griffin and Leo have been gone two days.

I looked up through the branches to see what time of day it was and glimpsed black clouds racing by. High up in the canopy, treetops are getting whipped around, yet down here there's no wind.

I chuck some wood on the embers. Smoke darts a tongue out from under the wood, licking its sides, squirming up into the air; a flame wriggles into existence, vanishes, wriggles, vanishes. Raindrops begin to hit the fire, making it hiss. If there was a storm yesterday, I was too out of it to notice. I hope Griffin and Leo are on land, waiting for the storm to pass. I hope that's the explanation.

I'll say one thing: reading is an act that should definitely take place between two minds. Reading your own writing is onanistic (a word I learned in Sunday school) and embarrassing. It has none of the pleasure that normally comes with reading.

The fight scene with the mob over Leo's vehicle infraction, meeting Ruby, the goldfish—they're accurate but I left so much out. The part is made to stand for the whole, and then the part becomes the whole.

The memories I left out are already different from the ones I included; they've transformed and morphed. My journal has become a barricade, a closed border: the memories on the inside are uniform and almost foreign to me, the ones on the outside are smoky and intimate; the ones on the inside are like the army, and the ones on the outside are like guerilla fighters.

I am apprehensive about reading to the end. Things are bad enough without stirring up that pot. I might not.

I am going for water. Griffin said the creek isn't far. I don't want to bust my stitches or bleed again so I'm only taking two empties.

I'm wearing three sweaters under my coat. I wrapped a T-shirt around my head, eased a knit hat over that, and tied the hat on with a scarf under my chin. I'm wearing two pairs of pants with a third wrapped around my neck. I'm carrying the knife open. I will advance while slowly turning 360 degrees. I would have painted a face on the back of my hat—cougars prefer to attack from the rear—but lack the means. I'll be scanning for changes in sound, smell, air pressure.

My face felt her. She was watching. I felt her presence the way you know when a woman is looking at you. My stitches burned. I had to walk out into the river to a place deep enough to fill the bottles. I was completely exposed. I drained a bottle, refilled it, filled the other.

The birds weren't silent, but they didn't sound relaxed either. She was there, but I didn't think she was hunting me. She was just watching. It bothers me that she can see me but

I never see her. I'm sure she's killed something else. That's why I'm getting a rest.

Four days. If they don't return soon, I'll have to go on alone. I'm about a quarter the way up Vancouver Island, maybe more. I'll head for the cabin rather than going back and hope to find them there.

It's still very windy. In these waters hypothermia sets in in half an hour. That boy Griffin is something special. My brother is the usual lunatic.

I heard a scream. A wildcat did howl.

I check and recheck the knife, mentally rehearsing.

I finished reading my old journal. I've found a kind of peace. My strategy must've worked, though truthfully, I don't know how.

I will find Ruby if I return. There is one sure place to look. February 21, at Molly's grave.

I heard the scream again. I leapt up, knife in hand, thinking the cougar might be attacking Griffin and Leo as they were walking up from the beach. She screamed again and I realized the sound was coming from behind me, away from the sea. And then I heard another scream, not hers, same distance. A series of yowls finished with another scream. She must be mating. She must be at the end of weaning.

A small part of me travels in her now: a scrap of my right upper lip, some scalp, my blood.

I was taking out the stitches—pack propped up against a tree, rectangle of mirror on top—and had taken out three or four when I heard a twig snap and a small thump. I put the scissors down and picked up the knife and turned, back against the tree. The thump could have been the sound of a heavy cat jumping out of a tree, hitting the forest floor.

The river should be behind us, Griffin called to Leo. I called out to them. They arrived in camp within a minute.

Hey bro. Less like hamburger, more like tripe, Leo said as he strode across the clearing.

They'd been blown way out into the strait by the wind and had paddled through the night trying to get back. Exhausted, they had gone ashore at the first land they reached, assuming they were on Vancouver Island. When they woke, they realized they were on a smaller island. Wind and exhaustion prevented them from leaving. They stayed on the island another night, eating the fish they'd caught. It had taken two full days in the chop to find the upright paddle that marked our landing point.

Griffin got me to sit down, took the scissors, and started to carefully snip and pull.

The next day we left. The wind was blowing northeast up the strait, which was excellent because I was weak. My back muscles burned, my head pounded, and my wounds ached. Leo had to stop frequently and wait for us to catch up.

Despite my discomfort, I was uncommonly happy to be back on the northern waters, moving over the strait's dark surface. Every time I raised my paddle, icy seawater trickled onto my hands. Cold briny air filled my lungs. Jellyfish billowed and propelled below the surface.

We remarked on how few seabirds there were. The herring run, if it even happens anymore, would have been long over, but even so, the number of birds was small. We saw a few northern gulls walking on tidal flats and once we heard the peeping of sandpipers. A mini-flock of Canada Geese, five birds strong, flew overhead and we stopped paddling to watch.

Late in the day, as the evening mist rose on the water, we heard a sound like chainsaws starting. We slowed and peered ahead. To the starboard came a sigh, followed by a ripple. Seconds later, on the port side a huffing erupted, like a dog warming a scent with its breath, and a few metres ahead, another large sigh. The water's surface broke.

Sea lions, Griffin whispered and grinned.

A large head appeared between the boats. I could see its coat was light brown. Several other heads surfaced and came round the boats, huffing. They were massive.

I'm getting the feeling they want us to leave, Griffin whispered.

We were gliding toward a small island of grass and rock covered with dark bodies. We began to paddle backward slowly, then angled away out to sea. Killer whales are thought to be extinct and we'd seen no seals. The sea lions were a privilege.

Nirvana is on the northern inside curve of a small peninsula on the east of Vancouver Island called the Forgotten Peninsula. The shape is unmistakable on a map—Leo and I always called it the penis-ula. When our family bought the place, an elderly couple from the K'omoks people were still paddling out every spring for a few weeks to camp and harvest shellfish. They stopped coming when I was about ten. My mother told us that all the broken shells in the sandy dirt were called a midden and that the piles of shells probably dated back thousands of years, way before the Roman Empire and ancient Greece. Leo and I had looked for cool stuff like bones, arrowheads, and slave killers, but never found any. Even three feet down, the shells were thick as ever.

The base of the peninsula, where it attaches to the main island, is no more than thirty metres wide and mostly blocked by a huge rock that my father believed to be a meteorite, leaving an entrance only fifty centimetres wide at high tide—just wide enough for an adult to pass without getting their feet wet. We used to park the car at the end of the dirt road and hike in all our provisions. Leo and I joked about how the mighty member was hanging on by a thread and played out disastrous scenarios of it getting an erection.

Leo said we were close to the cabin as the crow flies, but because of the peninsula and the bluffs on the south, it was still a half day's paddle away. Night was falling so we made camp and ate a potage of lentils, rice, salt, and a small fish that Griffin had caught trolling in the one-seater. Leo divvied it up. Griffin looked at his bowl with dissatisfaction. Leo had given himself the lion's share. My appetite still hasn't returned so I gave Griffin some of mine despite his protests.

Hungry boy, Leo commented. I paddled solo today, brother. You could throw me some too.

Griffin's portion was a bit light.

Oh? Was it? So sorry, my boy. He reached over and ruffled Griffin's hair.

Leo shovelled in the rest of his bowl, looking at Griffin.

When we arrived at Nirvana I was weak and feverish. The wind had switched and blew hard against us, and rounding the peninsula had been difficult. No one realized how weak I was until I fell in the water getting out of the kayak and was unable to stand back up. Leo and Griffin helped me onto land, pulled the boats up, and shouldered me up the hill to the cabin. The door was unlocked and the house smelled like mint tea. The fact that I'd smelled chicken manure and wafts of other livestock while walking up registered now. A place was set at the kitchen table—knife, fork, plate, and glass on Mom's yellow plasticized tablecloth.

Someone's here, Leo whispered. My heart leapt with the hope it was one of the boys, but the neat single setting suggested something else. They led me to the daybed in the sunroom. Griffin put a blanket over me and I whispered, Tell me what you find out.

I woke to sounds from the kitchen, a serious-toned female voice and Leo's voice, reassuring. I called out and they came.

This is Parker. Parker Leclerc. Griffin introduced me to a tall, physically strong young woman with brown braided hair, eyes that moved quickly. She looked like she was almost certainly pregnant.

She's been living here for months, he said. She's put in a garden and she's raising chickens and goats.

Leo came in and said, It's bloody Goldilocks and the three bears.

Parker looked at my wounds and left. She returned with clean linen and a hot damp towel. Griffin changed the bed and helped me undress. I slept for twenty hours. A deep twenty. I hadn't felt so warm and safe since I was a kid. Being back in the family home was total surrender, like dying, the good version.

The next few days I woke, ate, drank, and sank back into the warmth and the quiet. I asked Parker if she had seen any trace of my boys when she arrived. All the supplies I had laid in were gone, and the rifle and ammunition and all the water purification kits, gone also, but she said there was nothing to indicate who'd taken them.

She asked if we'd seen many people on our journey up. A few people digging clams, I answered. A few people fishing, an occasional chimney with smoke coming out. Mostly near towns—Nanaimo, Courtenay/Comox, Campbell River. How about here? Anyone living around here?

Not that I've seen, she answered.

One day I woke to a loud clatter. I made my way to the kitchen where the noise was coming from and found Leo on his hands and knees, pulling out all the pots and pans from the cupboard under the electrical wall oven. He held up a desiccated mouse by the tail.

Must've been poisoned by Mom, what, thirty years ago.

What are you doing?

Glad you're feeling better.

Yep.

I went over to the woodstove and opened the door. The feel of the worn wooden handle in my hand was instantly familiar, like putting on an old shoe. I could picture my parents' hands holding it as they threw in another chunk of wood and I felt the layers of their grip under mine.

I looked up and saw, hanging on a hook, the metal rod for lifting the eyes of the woodstove. It was attached by a leather thong, and I thought about the fact that that thong, that thin piece of animal hide, had outlasted two living, breathing, full-bodied adults, and then I thought how many of the things around me would continue to exist when I was gone, and discovered that was a good feeling.

Are you okay? my brother asked.

I nodded and filled the kettle.

I'm reorganizing the cupboards.

You're kidding me.

No. We're going to be here for a while, and I thought I might as well get things organized.

He went outside and tossed the mouse into the bush. Never say people don't change.

I woke to the sound of my old guitar and it flooded me with a laughing/crying feeling remembering summers of fun, fun, fun, when everything was still pretty good in my world. The old man was working on the base and Mom would feed us meals whenever we were hungry, leaving Leo and me free to play until the sun set late at night. The days were warm and sunny and harmless.

I called out to see who was playing. Griffin came into the sunroom. He had found a supply of new strings and replaced the broken ones. I asked him to keep playing. He laughed sheepishly and strummed a few bars of a couple of songs, each time falling away apologetically. How is it I never knew he played so well? Crap uncle.

I sat up and tried myself. The last thirty years hadn't exactly loosened up my fingers. I played the opening chords of the first song I made up. *Like bees around a flower, Like a dog around a bone, you and I hit puberty, and now we're on the pho-o-o-ne. I put my arms around you, and planted my first kiss.*

Leo came in from the living room singing, *I'll be coming back for more girl, that's a thrill I'm gonna miss.* I remember that, he said. I thought it was sheer genius. I thought you were going to make a million. Wow.

It's good to be here. An eagle called out by the ocean and I heard an echo of my mother's laugh. The memories are good and the place is beautiful and largely undamaged by the catastrophes. We lost a grove of cedar trees, a small chunk of land eroded into the sea at the north-eastern tip, and the beach is almost gone, but on the plus side, the access to the peninsula from the main island is almost gone too. We're all glad to be here. Leo and Griffin look more or less relaxed. We all like Parker. Leo and Griffin gave her all our supplies—we had enough to last a couple of months—and put her in charge of doling out the food. Griffin's going to fish and Parker's excited about the possibility, with all of us here, of digging up a field and planting crops. She thinks there's still time in the season.

She came in from the kitchen where I could smell one of her soups cooking, drying her hands on a tea towel Mom had embroidered during one of her crafty periods. I picked out the opening notes for "Come as You Are."

I used to think our parents called this place after the band, I said.

What did they call it after? Parker asked.

While the band used the name ironically, I imagine, my mother was full-on serious. She never lost the hippie side of herself, even when she married a guy in the military.

It's an Indian word for heaven, I said. Freedom from suffering and desire.

Griffin said, I always felt happy here. At home. I miss Gran. He glanced at Leo.

I remember the feeling of endless time, I said, and feeling free. Too free maybe. Remember, Leo, when we bought weed from that guy at the cove and we took the boat out with the wakeboard you made in woodshop and it completely came apart? You almost drowned we were laughing so hard.

Remember when the drug squad 'copter buzzed real low over Waterstone's and we waited for an hour, then went to check it out and the cops had loaded up all the plants from the bust in the back of their van and left the doors wide open? We pulled up, Leo said to Parker and Griffin, and I don't know where the cops were but they weren't there. We stuffed as much as we could into Mom's hatchback and took off. Then we heard the helicopter following us and we freaked. Luckily, Allen remembered the big maple tree at Hasek's so we tore in under the canopy, unloaded everything, brushed out all the leaves and twigs with a T-shirt, I think, and took off back down the highway. We drove for half an hour until the 'copter veered away. They pulled us over later, but they had no proof.

Yeah, I smiled. I definitely remember that.

That little prank started me on the road to success. And you, Leo sneered happily at me, wanted to give it all away.

I noodled away at a few chords. I'd forgotten I was partly to blame for your life of crime. I laughed. Where was my cut then? Did I ever get anything?

A lifetime's supply of free dope as I recall, risk-free.

Leo looked out the window at the old rope swing strung between two firs. I wonder if we could grow any now, he said. Did I stash any seeds? Goldilocks, you seen any plants that looked like weed growing out there? Do you even know what they look like? She shook her head. Bro, let's check it out tomorrow. The clearing in the scrotum. Maybe there's something. Maybe I can even find my old bong. That would be the ticket, eh?

Parker is five or six months' pregnant. It can be harder to tell in taller women. She seems happy to have company, though the three-guys-one-woman dynamic is not ideal. Griffin seems definitely interested, helping her work in the garden, helping her cook, doing the clean-up. Leo also seems interested. His focus intensifies when she's in the room.

Yesterday I was looking through Mom's bookshelf in the living room before dinner and heard Parker in the hallway. Not so fast, monsieur.

Time is short, madam, Leo said, his voice thick and low.

Not for me it isn't, she said.

She walked toward the kitchen. Leo waited a couple of seconds then followed at a trot. On the scent. Then at dinner tonight Leo came into the kitchen transformed. He'd cut his hair to an inch long around his head and trimmed his beard close to his face. The removal of so much gray hair had a startling effect. First off, he looks more sane, though his blue eyes are still too intense. Second, he looks younger, almost a generation younger, granddad to silverback, and he looks handsome, I suppose, compact, experienced, fit, hyper-alert. Griffin's soft-hued, quietly perceptive blue eyes, clear skin, and mop of reddish-brown curls probably look boyish in comparison.

We were already sitting at the table when Leo came in. He raised his hand in a flourish toward Parker and said, Hey there, Lady Madonna, looking beautiful!

Parker laughed in that practiced way women seem to develop, acknowledging a compliment without giving anything back.

You're too kind, she said and snapped the elastic waist of an old pair of men's track pants. If you can say that while I'm wearing these. You guys are going to be seeing a lot of these track pants until bébé comes.

They never looked better! And I like your hair like that.

Parker bugged her eyes out at Leo. Her hair was a tangled mess.

Hey, Leo turned his hands palm upward, I like the wild look.

As a man looking at another guy's efforts at seduction, it's always hard to see how women ever say yes. They must perceive something we don't, like a dog whistle; there must be a frequency, undetectable to the male of the species, that we somehow nonetheless generate. Leo actually seemed to be making headway.

Griffin must have been thinking similar thoughts.

Could you get any cornier? he asked.

Parker looked at Griffin and he looked down at his cup and swirled his tea leaves into a whirlpool. His shoulders were hunched. He glanced up at her, ignoring his stepfather, then put his cup down and left.

I could almost see the calculations going on in the back of Parker's mind for her baby, herself, the dangers over the next few years, what she was going to need, and I could see her body starting to respond.

That was one of the things I'd loved about Ruby. Our connection had nothing to do with survival, with numbers or calculation.

Last night Griffin went to the well for water and rushed back in. Three shooting stars. We ran out and saw four streak across the sky, two short ones, a long bright arc, and a faint one low on the horizon. It's been a long time since I looked at a night sky with no clouds. The big dipper was there and the Milky Way, and it seemed strange that the sky hadn't changed while everything down here on earth had.

Our necks got tired so we lay on the ground and called them out to each other, oohing and ahhing at the more spectacular ones. Parker said she felt the baby doing somersaults and flips. It was one of those rare occasions when four people feel more or less the same way—happy and lucky.

We got cold on the ground. Griffin had the idea to pull our mattresses and blankets outside. I suggested we lay a tarp underneath. Soon we lay side by side, our feet slightly slanted down the slope, getting warm and drowsy, chatting, dropping off one by one.

I woke several times during the night, my hand or shoulder cold, and saw a wisp of cloud passing in front of the stars or the maple tree in silhouette or another bright chip of white slide down the sky, vanishing, leaving behind millions and billions of stars whose current existence was unknown.

On one of the occasions that I woke I heard Leo roll over, and I whispered, Hey, bro, you awake?

Grunt.

Thanks, I said

What for?

Getting me up here.

Yeah.

I'm making a bow and arrow and leg snares. Griffin and I went fishing last night in the rowboat with a flashlight. I felt okay. We caught a rock cod. The only thing Leo is doing is cleaning out cupboards.

Of all of us, including the wreck that is me, Leo is by far the most restless.

The cougar has rolled me back to the animal world, where survival is not a moral issue. The smell of her fur, the weight of her paw, the warmth of my blood running down my face—some of the fight had already gone out of me. Before Griffin turned around I was getting ready to surrender my soul.

Last night we sat at the table after a feast of roasted rabbit in a shallow broth with onions, carrots, parsley seeds, and oregano cooked in Mom's old turkey roasting pan that I found in the shed. The candlelight made everyone's eyes look bright. We opened the door to the wood burning stove and basked in the heat and orange light.

Ahh, Leo said. Life on the big dick as we used to say, back in the day.

We've already got our regular places at the table. Parker sits beside Griffin near the door. Leo sits across from Parker with his back to the sink and I'm beside Leo across from Griffin. Parker eats with her elbows on the table, usually holding her head up with one hand. She keeps her chair back a few centimetres from the table and her feet on the floor. When she's finished she pushes her chair back farther, lays one foot on the knee of her other leg, and leans back.

Griffin eats in a careful, measured way, like a young man who has been taught excellent table manners. I struggle with my injured lip—concentrating on keeping the food in my mouth and not looking gross. Leo is tucked in close to the table so he can reach whatever he wants—the water jug, salt dish, second helpings. You'd never believe we were from the same family, his table manners are so bad. He chews with his mouth open and rolls the food around from one side to the other, snorting and smacking and picking his teeth as he goes. He uses his fingers to eat whenever possible, then licks them clean one at a time, flourishing each one toward whoever cooked the meal, as though his gestures were a compliment. Food attaches itself to his beard and moustache and he leaves it there, it seems, out of spite. I'm tired of handing him a napkin he never uses. His eating style might explain why Parker pushes away from the table as soon as she can.

Don't you wish you could eat a good old spicy Spanish sausage? Leo asked the table. He seemed uncharacteristically happy and relaxed. Or chocolate? Or coffee?

Bubblegum! said Parker.

We might get coffee again, said the ever-cup-half-full Griffin. The green line to Mexico is almost finished. It'll cost a few days' rations, of course—we'll be able to drink like one cup a month, but eventually prices should come down.

The crowd in my head turned over in graves they never had. Coffee exports.

167

A good bottle of wine, said Leo.

Driving a motorcycle, said Griffin.

Hot tubs, Parker said.

Hockey, added Griffin.

I miss hopping on a plane and leaving everything behind. Walking out the door of a five-star into tropical heat and a smell like ripe mangos. Beaches full of women in bikinis.

I didn't speak. What was I going to say? Beaches? Don't you wish you could have your old life back? Your wife? Your family? I would have been a downer. I smiled at everyone else's whimsy.

This OneWorld crap, Leo reared his chair on its hind legs. I guess it won't be over in my lifetime.

I have to give him credit. He has a real instinct for keeping a pleasant conversation rolling along.

It's working right now, he said, but it won't last. It goes against our nature. We're bean counters. We keep track of who gets what and who does what. We get severely pissed off at the assholes who don't do their share. You watch. People are just biding their time. When the fear wanes, all this cooperation shit will morph back into competition. Socialism—nice idea, but it doesn't work.

I was chewing on a rabbit leg, pinning every shred of meat between my incisors and tugging it off, watching Leo, who was speaking to the air above the table. Parker looked at her knife. Griffin was stabbing his fork into a crack in the table.

You know, Leo, Griffin said, capitalism, nice idea, but it doesn't work either. Leads to socialism every time.

We have a taker, Leo held his hand out in welcome. And that works vice versa, I might add. Socialism, he turned his hands up. Capitalism.

Griffin kept digging at the table crack. Life *is* better now. Maybe for some people it'll be hard having only one kid, but that'll only last two, maybe three generations, and besides, it makes everyone family now.

When the effects of the die-off settle and we start generating wealth again, you'll see, it'll be business as usual. Quick, he snapped his fingers, as a broker's keystroke.

Those days are gone forever, Griffin countered. The model of eternal economic growth is finished. It was a mass delusion, created for the few to hoard a lot. No one is going to buy into that anymore. It defies the laws of nature. Maybe there's a few holdouts in your generation, old wavers who can't make the adjustment, but does my generation look unhappy? Do we look like we want to go back to your world? No. We get by, we work hard, have fun, make music, get drunk on occasion, smoke a little herb, and try not to mess each other up. Friends, Leo, ever heard of friends? Besides, there is no world if we go back to the old one. And my generation, unlike yours, wants to live.

The scar tissue on my scalp tingled.

Not just your generation, I said at the same time as Leo answered, Wow. The excitement of the "life"—he made air quotes around the word—you anticipate is killing me. In fact, I guess it almost has. Leo looked at me and grinned, whiskers gleaming with rabbit fat.

There's behaviour that has a future, Griffin said, and behaviour that doesn't. It's easy to tell the difference. Everyone knows the difference.

A future? A bunch of Rasta boy scouts jamming their do-good lives away? No one controls the future. You can quote me on that.

At least we're not all—If I can just cram all this money into the bank I'll be safe forever. You call that excitement? You call that living? And by the way, Dermy, speaking of bean counters and people not doing their share. Griffin gave a bitter laugh. Not a dish! Not a vegetable! Not a finger on the broom or the stacking of a log. You too good for it? Now I know what my mom must've felt like.

Dermy? I hadn't heard that nickname. Leo's middle name is Dermid. I wanted to lighten the tone. I keep forgetting that I only know Griffin because he's Leo's stepson and that Griffin lived with Leo and Evie until he was a teenager.

If you were ruler of the world, Parker asked Leo carefully, concentrating, what would you have done? Something had to be done, didn't it? Or we'd all be dead? Extinct?

Leo shrugged. Maybe we needed to put on the brakes. Go through a cleanse or something. But not forever. Definitely not for fucking ever. OneWorld is not a new religion. It's a government. There's nothing new under the sun. The only thing I believe in is my life. My choices. Everything else is guesswork.

We have to try, don't we? We have to try and change.

A wee bit of a hypocrite, aren't you? Leo nodded at her belly. Not your first, I'll wager.

It was an accident.

And?

My first child was taken by his father.

I understand. But still, the planet ...

Everyone went silent.

Well, well, I didn't mean for everyone to get so solemn, Leo said, leaning back in his chair. I'd be doing just what you're doing. I certainly would.

Parker began to cry. I'm not going to kill it. I'd rather die. The baby can have my place.

Griffin shot a look at Leo.

No, Parker put her hand on Griffin's arm. I know it's wrong. If everyone acted like me, our species wouldn't survive. I don't have the right to be an exception. I know it. I'm not one of those who are resisting the law. I think the law is right. Meanwhile the baby is growing and I can't kill it. What hope is there?

Goodness gracious me! I said, mimicking our grandmother. If it comes to that, the baby can have my place. To tell you the truth, I haven't enjoyed life much for twenty years now, with the exception of the last few months.

Leo looked sharply at me. Then he eased his chair back on its hind legs and said, This all started with my saying I'd like a spicy Spanish sausage. Lighten up, folks. I expect you'll give birth to a beautiful baby, and even I will make like a socialist and help it flourish. He toasted an invisible glass in her direction.

Parker sat without moving, then said she was tired and went to bed. Griffin followed.

Not bad for one evening's work, I said.

He leaned forward and put his elbows on the table. But look at the pair of us. Neither one really caring if we live. What would the parents think?

I was thinking that Parker would have to be watched closely after she had that baby. I was thinking I was going to have to find an argument to get her off the hook with herself.

Our parents? They'd be happy we were here.

Well, you anyway.

I wanted to change the subject. I remembered his original pitch for coming up here. By the way, I said, when should we deal with Mom and Dad's ashes? Where should we put them?

Let's help Parker get the field established and the seeds planted first. Let's get everything in place for next winter before we think about that.

I stared at the fire thinking how I couldn't live without the idea that the world was going to get better in some way, and by "world," I meant humans. By better I wasn't thinking about progress or technology, obviously, but maybe about evolution. I don't know, but my whole adult life I've always been checking the pulse of our country, our culture, our species. I'd never thought of it as a compulsion before, but it is; I need that sense of underlying purpose. Part of being a soldier maybe. Without that, the emptiness is unbearable. I'm the flip side of Leo. And nothing like Griffin.

I had an attack of vertigo this morning. Went back to bed.

I can't shake the feeling that something is up with Leo. I don't know what it is. I'm watching, listening for clues.

Late spring and we're clearing and ploughing. Trying to get a field ready for planting in the first week of June. The three of us. Parker wants to help, but none of us want that baby to come early. She's taking care of seed plants in the greenhouse, plus the goats and the chickens. We made a plough using a large, sharp stone and arbutus branches tied together. Mostly Leo and Griffin stand on either side and push against a yoke and, because of my peg leg, I guide the angled piece with the stone attached. It's tricky work because Leo and Griffin have to push hard to get the damn thing moving and stop whenever we hit a stone. Then we dig the stone out and carry it to clearance cairns every five metres or so. Also we have to chop down alder that have sprung up in the years since dad last cleared the land and dig out the stumps. Burn piles are illegal, so we drag everything to the field's edge. I don't like the messy visuals and want to drag the debris further into the bush, but Leo and Griffin voted me down. We're leaving a tree every couple of metres for shade.

Dad hired a guy with a backhoe to make this field; he had the idea of putting in his own driving range. I don't think he ever sprang for the net, but Leo and I remembered him whacking cheap balls into the forest and me yelling Fore! and Leo yelling Skin! The first time one turned up when we were working in the field, I was confused, thinking I'd uncovered some kind of tuber or egg that was going to hatch something, and I just couldn't remember what.

Digging up the old golf balls dredged up other stuff from the distant past. When we were kids we used to play with Mom's pile of sea soil for her garden. We used her gardening trowel and I'd fill Leo's dump truck with my backhoe and Leo would drive it over somewhere and make a big pile. We made encampments out of sticks and stones and staged battles with plastic soldiers Mom got at the dollar store. We played with those soldiers for days without getting bored.

Once we stole my sister Lucy's Barbie from her bedroom. She never used it. She was practically still a baby. It must have been a gift from someone. When we first took the doll, we pretended Barbie was driving the truck, but that lasted about a millisecond. We stuck her pointy legs in the dirt and ran her over with the truck and the backhoe. The sea soil had plenty of worms and we watched in fascination as a worm slid over her nipple-less breasts and disappeared into the ground beneath. This triggered some kind of frenzy in us and we pulled her legs and arms off and threw the parts into the bushes.

Our sister died not long afterward. We both felt like we'd called forth some kind of horrible voodoo spell with the destruction of the Barbie and for a long time that guilt shadowed our sadness.

Looking back, I think we never felt quite as easy with each other after that.

After Lucy's death (our parents told us years later that it was inoperable brain cancer), my father was sharp with Leo and tensed whenever he came into the room. And I remember Leo started flinching when our mother hugged him, like he didn't believe her anymore, or like she was trying to imprison him, or he knew he didn't deserve it.

We've settled into a rhythm. The three of us go to the field after breakfast and work hard until mid-afternoon. Parker shows up around eleven with water and food and surveys what we've done, checking out where the sun is reaching. She takes a hoe and plants seeds where we've worked and stakes poles with shiny material to discourage birds from eating the seedlings. When she finds a slug she pierces its body with a sharp stick and we all find something humorous in her pregnant viciousness.

We cleared the field. We ploughed it quickly a second time, unsettling any weeds and grass that were starting to lay roots again. We're half-way through planting carrots, tomatoes, spinach, garlic, potatoes, and onions. Parker wants us to plant some wheat to keep her seed base strong. With all the rain, drainage is our problem, not irrigation.

Every night we sit down for dinner tired and happy. Last night, though, there was a moment. Griffin reached out and touched Parker's cheek while she was talking and she just kept on talking like it was normal. Leo noticed.

Leo's moved onto "organizing" the sideboard in the living room. The floor's covered with old bills, chipped crockery, printouts of grade-twelve English lesson plans, a Nintendo Game Boy, boxes of photos of relatives from Mom's side. I cannot imagine Leo cares about any of it.

You looking for something? I ask.

He stood up. I'm wondering where a few things are. He held his hands oddly, with the thumb and forefinger of one hand pincering the webby flesh between the thumb and forefinger of the other.

Like what? I looked around.

He squeezed harder.

A thought entered into my head. I asked him, The will?

He shifted his grip so his thumbnail dug into the flesh of the other hand.

Whatever they wrote, I said, it won't make any difference now. There aren't even lawyers for this stuff anymore.

He released his hand. That, he said slowly, would be what you would say. Of course it won't make any fucking difference to *you*. Why would it? I want to see what our parents said. What difference does *that* make to you?

Leo showed up at breakfast this morning with something weighty in his coat pocket. It clanked against the table when he sat down. We stopped eating and looked at him.

What?

What've you got? I asked.

A tool.

What tool?

A wrench.

A wrench?

I found it in the attic.

And kept it in your pocket?

You never know.

It's not a wrench is it?

No?

It's a gun, isn't it?

Ooh. You're good.

Show her here.

It was wrapped in a piece of flannel. A Browning Hi-Power 9mm. Unloaded.

Did you find cartridges?

Leo ate his porridge. Let me eat my breakfast will you?

Where did you find it?

In the attic. I told you.

So, yesterday?

He shrugged. When he finished breakfast, he held his hand out for the gun. I didn't want to give it to him.

I was lying around after a late afternoon doze watching the sun make shadows on the ceiling and imagining Ruby seeing my new face. The gold-green flecks in her eyes, the corners of her wide mouth turning up. She'd like this new look: same Allen Quincy but topped with oddly angled tufts of hair, a raised, jagged red scar along the hairline, the clear markings of a claw on my left cheek, and the missing bit of lip. I was imagining her walking around the corner into my room when Griffin and Parker came pounding up the back porch stairs and threw open the screen door.

There's a dead deer, Parker said.

A fresh kill, Griffin added. Only part of the chest cavity has been eaten.

My heart quickened.

I'm scared, Parker said.

Of course.

No, I'm really scared.

Where is it? I asked.

Just the other side of the meteor. Parker can't be outside alone anymore. Not until we know it's gone.

I can't say why, but I was happy. I believed it had to be the same cougar. I felt that she'd come back for me. I wanted to see her again.

Cougars maintain a big range, I said. It won't stay long. Besides, they're shy.

One attacked you, Parker said.

A cripple.

I want the gun, Parker said.

Have you talked to Leo?

They shook their heads.

Cougars come from behind. You won't even know it's there. You won't know what's hit you. A gun won't help. A knife would be better.

I'll stay with Parker. It won't attack two of us.

That boy, I thought, is a sweetie-pie, as my mother used to say.

I'd like Griffin to have the gun then, Parker said.

He's just as likely to shoot you as the cat if it jumps you.

We were all at the table. Oyster stew. The sound of spoons clinking on bowls. Slurps. Parker told Leo about the kill. The hair stands up on the back of my neck even going to the outhouse, she said. I keep turning around and trying to see into the bushes.

Maybe stay inside for a couple of days, Leo suggested. It'll move on once it's finished the deer.

It's probably been here for years, I said. I agree. It's going to finish its kill and move on.

Leo looked at me. You think it could be the same one?

It could be. They range up to 160 kilometres. How far away was our campsite?

Sixty, seventy kilometres.

I want the gun until it goes away, Parker interrupted.

A knife is better, Leo said. I'll lend you my knife.

Griffin looked at Parker and said, We probably wouldn't use the gun, but we'd feel safer.

Leo spooned a few mouthfuls in while he considered whether to answer.

I'd feel safer keeping it, he said. If I thought it would be useful, I'd be only too happy. Surely you agree Allen?

About the cougar, yes, but I think the pistol belongs to the house and should be left in a kitchen drawer with the cartridges so if any of us need it we can get it. Also I'd like to give Griffin and Parker basic shooting lessons. Without using bullets obviously.

I've come to like having it, Leo said and leaned back on his chair. Does it really matter? He stretched his arms over his head. Who's going to come here?

Who knows what's going to happen. I'd like to give them lessons.

I can give them lessons. I'm as experienced with this weapon as you.

No you're not. I'm a soldier

You *were* a soldier. Twenty years go.

How about they pick their teacher?

How about we stop talking about this shit.

He put his head down close to his bowl and spooned the last of his stew in.

You find what you're looking for yet? I asked.

Am I looking for something?

I threw my spoon in my empty bowl and pushed my chair back. My blood was starting to boil. Nothing like a brother.

I was up first in the morning. I started a fire, milked the goat, and made the oatmeal and tea, then tiptoed into Griffin's room to wake him up. I don't know why but I was surprised to see Parker in the bed with him. I wondered how long that had been going on and whether Leo was aware of it.

I touched his shoulder, mimed that I wanted to talk, and tiptoed out. He came out in boxers, carrying his clothes and shoes, and followed me to the kitchen. I'd never seen his body before. His skin was very pale. His shoulders were broad but the muscle wasn't defined.

I want you to show me the carcass, I whispered.

Sure ... Griffin hopped on one foot as his other struggled to find a way through the leg of his pants. Only one problem. Well, at least one.

Yeah?

Parker. She doesn't want to be left alone with Leo.

I let that sink in.

Because of the pistol?

No.

He did up his pants, then sat down and pulled up his socks. In my mind I replayed overhearing Leo making a move on Parker.

She doesn't trust him, Griffin said.

Sure, bring her, but she can't make a sound. I want to keep Leo out of it. I want to see the cougar alone.

We walked quietly, Griffin in the front, Parker in the middle, knives drawn. We filed past the meteor and headed up the slope of the mountain. Griffin sighted the carcass. It had been dragged partially into the underbrush, head and fore hooves poking out into the open. The bone buds of its antlers were just erupting. The eyes were cloudy and ringed with flies. Inside the brambles you could make out the red hollow of the chest cavity with flashes of white bone and tendon and you could see a claw mark on its back. Griffin and Parker both thought it had been moved since the day before. Griffin crouched down, peered into the bush and said that a large portion of the hindquarters had also been eaten.

I told Griffin and Parker my plan. Griffin was not happy about it. I rubbed myself with dirt and leaves and fir nee-dles—under the armpits, the crotch, and scalp—to minimize my scent and threw a rope over the first branch and secured it. Climbing with the peg leg wasn't easy, but I braced my legs against the trunk and pulled myself up hand-over-hand until I reached the first branch. I pulled the rope up after me and coiled it, ready for a quick descent. I cut some suckers and tucked them through my belt, then hoisted myself up onto the next branch. The branches higher up were not sturdy enough to hold a cougar's body. It could only ap-proach from below. I lay down and arranged the suckers to camouflage myself, with Griffin's help. I had two knives and a whistle. I would've appreciated the pistol, but screw it.

Griffin hovered below, unwilling to leave me alone. I told him I'd faced much worse than a fifty-five-plus kilo cat and it wasn't going to catch me by surprise this time.

Why do you want to see it so much? he fretted.

Curiosity.

Killed the cat, Parker whispered automatically. You don't have a death wish do you?

Make space for the baby? I said and grinned. I've got the whistle. If you hear it send Leo with the Browning.

The light shifted across the forest floor as hours passed. The deer's head strained away from its neck.

Mid-morning I was meditating on the neon-yellow-green of new leaves when, from the corner of my eye, I saw the carcass move. Without moving my head I refocused on the deer. The cougar had materialized in the clearing. She could have been the one that attacked me, based on Griffin's description. Same size, same age, same slack belly. She got the buck by the scruff of the neck and tugged it into the clearing, the muscles on her haunches taut with effort. She bobbed her head a few times, sniffed at the gut, then lay down and ate from the haunch. Presently she yawned and burbled and a young male trotted into the clearing. He came over to her and nuzzled her under the chin until she batted him away. He was followed by two slightly smaller cubs, females I assumed.

After eating her fill the mother moved a short distance away and lay down where I couldn't see her. Her offspring moved in to eat, growling at each other when one got too close to the other's feeding place. The young male finished first and headed toward his mother but soon returned and started to eat right beside one of his sisters, who yowled and flattened her ears but didn't stop eating. The male didn't move. His sister swatted him, looking in their mother's direction.

The male eventually stopped eating and skittered toward the trunk of my tree. I worried he was going to climb it—I hadn't factored in offspring—but he lay down in the shade beneath me and started to groom. I wondered if the movement from my breathing would catch his eye. Eventually a huffing sound came from the mother and all the young stopped and looked at her.

The carcass moved back toward the bush. She must've come round under the bushes to pull it in because I couldn't see anything. The young disappeared into the bush one after the other. I waited a long time, then lowered the rope down, waited another interval, then eased myself down.

Walking home I felt emptied out and filled up at the same time. I wanted to return the next day to watch her. I was mesmerized.

Then I thought of Parker and the baby and Griffin and Leo back at the house without me and sped up. I no longer liked the thought of the three of them there without me.

The air had lost the last traces of morning damp and the temperature was rising. I got a noseful of ocean as I walked past the meteor onto our peninsula, the incoming tide picking up whatever had died at low tide—crabs, mussels, sea worms—and wafting their scent inland with the breeze. Ravens cawed excitedly. For a moment, as I stood in the warm sun, the world seemed a perfect place. Then the sun started to burn.

I returned to the kill site the next morning, excited. As I approached I noticed turkey vultures in the trees. The carcass had been pulled out into the clearing and was picked clean. I sat and stared at it until the pressure of the waiting vultures activated my departure. On my return to the cabin, I felt low.

I came in through the sun porch, lay on my bed, and started writing. The house is quiet. Leo and Griffin are probably working in the field. I'm thinking that the goats and chickens may not escape the cougars' notice for long. Four top-down predators are four too many.

Yesterday we discussed what to do about them. Leo was for killing them, but even Parker isn't enthusiastic about killing a mother and her cubs. Leo pointed out that they'd be full-grown soon. I said that would mean they'd strike out for their own territories, though I had to admit waiting that out didn't seem like much of a strategy. I reiterated that once the deer was eaten they'd probably leave. If they hung around I suggested we could scare them away. I actually suggested banging pot lids. Griffin took over at that point and said we should at least clear the brush from around the cabin, the goat pen and chicken coop, the outhouse and the kitchen garden, to eliminate hiding places.

The quiet around here is starting to bother me. I have a feeling of doom again, of things closing in, hanging by a thread, of this interval being some kind of pivot. I feel that what I do next could have bad repercussions if I fail to read the signs correctly.

Leo walked in on me as I was writing.

What's that?

I closed this journal.

He cocked his head. You keeping a list? Naughty and nice?

What do you want?

That's a little hostile, brother. I just came to talk about the cougars. I was hoping that upon reflection you weren't still endorsing the let's sit around and do fuck all approach.

I am.

Are you nuts? That thing attacked you, a grown man, with other men nearby. You have to believe it could try again. Parker isn't safe.

If it's the same one, Griffin managed to hit her hard with the frying pan, and she came away with nothing. She's going to think deer are easier prey.

If. Wouldn't it be more prudent to eliminate it? Even exciting? Kill the mother and the rest will scamper. I've never tasted cougar meat. Cat soup!

Do you even know who you're talking to? They've got as much right to be here as we do. They haven't harmed us.

Oh please. I'm going to vomit. You're a soldier for fuck's sake.

If it's the same one, it was me she attacked. I decide. I paused. I *was* a soldier remember, twenty years ago.

He looked at the journal, deciding if there was any reason to obey me.

Let me read your book.

No.

He looked out the open door. What did you do with your goldfish? I was wondering, what did Mr Pure and Noble do with his pets? Did he flush them down the toilet? Did he risk being busted and give them to someone to look after? Did he abandon them? What would Allen have done with those fish, I was asking myself?

I gave them to Velma at work. I put the pencil down on the bed, but held onto the journal. Odd you'd wonder.

Yeah, the things a person thinks about, eh? If those cougars hurt someone you're not going to feel all fucking Jane Goodall then.

I don't think you're particularly worried about them hurting someone.

Why did God burden me with such a sanctimonious, self-righteous prick of a brother? He smiled and left.

I smiled back because he was partly right. I could be a sanctimonious, self-righteous prick.

I stared at the spines of the books in front of me in the spalted alder bookshelf I'd made for Mom in woodworking, and the green cloth spines of *Treasure Island* and *Kidnapped* by Robert Louis Stevenson stood out, and with them came a memory of reading on the couch on a rainy afternoon, me on one couch with *Kidnapped* and Leo on the other with *Treasure Island*. He was eating cherries and he started lobbing them at me. I ate the ones he lobbed and spat the pits back at him. Idyllic, really.

The couches were upholstered in light green, I think, so Leo's cushion was soon covered in dark-red spots from the pits. Mom came through the living room on her way to the bedroom, smiling at first because we were laughing, and then she saw the stains.

Things got kind of strange then because she got angry with Leo but not with me, though clearly I was the main culprit. Leo started to cry and apologize, saying he'd save up and buy her new cushion covers. He begged her not to be mad anymore and I remember wishing Mom would just hug him or at least be mad at both of us, but she didn't soften.

When she left the room Leo stopped crying and turned his face into the cushion. I kept on reading and got back into the story. I didn't know what else to do. She'd sucked all the happiness out of the room.

What a memory.

I woke the next morning from a deep sleep surprised to be alive. I don't know why. Thinking about a river. Ruby's eyes. Birds chirping. Newness. Outside the window some of the tulips my mother and father planted twenty years ago are blooming. Wind ruffled the trees and the clouds were dark. I was savouring the warmth of bed when Parker pounded up the back steps.

A goat!

It had been missing when they went to water them. She and Griffin went to check the fishing net Parker had strung up across the peninsula access to keep deer out and had seen it just on the other side. I got dressed and we went together. It was three metres on the other side of the net. The wind was now thrashing the trees about.

It lay on its side, cold and stiffening. Its legs were slightly bent, the blood on its coat was coagulated and hardening. Its shoulder and chest were partially eaten. There was no blood on the ground around the body. I wondered how it had got past the net. Goats don't swim unless they have no choice. I couldn't see a cougar being able to jump the net while carrying the goat.

Griffin and I carried it back to the cabin, skinned and gutted it, cut around the eaten part. We salted and transferred most of the meat to the root cellar, except for what we roasted that evening.

The cougar is not going to be happy finding its carcass gone, Leo observed.

We have to try and kill them, Parker said.

They're going to go after goats and chickens way before they tackle a full-grown human, I said.

We need those goats and chickens, Parker said, turning on me.

If one attacks you, dear girl, Leo spoke while looking at me, what you do is jam your arm so far down its throat it starts to suffocate. It won't be able to bite down. You might get a scratch or two but you'll live. For the record, though, I agree. It's time to deal with them.

We're going to need the gun, Griffin said.

It's going to be useful. Yes.

I didn't like the way this conversation was going. I asked, Has anyone wondered how that goat ended up on the other side of the net?

The cougar carried it there for the cubs? Griffin suggested.

Really? Leapt over the net with the goat in its mouth? I don't even know if that's possible.

What are you suggesting? Leo sneered. An eagle?

I don't know how that goat got there, Parker said, and I don't care. We know cougars killed the deer, something killed the goat. I want them gone.

Leo looked at me. The shadow of a smile crossed his face.

I had the thought—Leo put the goat there. He killed it. Maybe to scare us. An act of terrorism. Maybe because he's bored and had an impulse to stir things up. Maybe he had a hankering for goat meat. Maybe he has no idea why he did it. I am not letting him kill those cougars. If they are around, I'll find a way to scare them off.

It took us two days to build a shed to keep the remaining goats in at night, and we're taking turns shepherding them during the day. Leo will not share the pistol he "found," which annoys the hell out of us. Griffin and I have to use a whistle, a knife, and spears we've made. Parker is accompanied everywhere outside. She's getting very big, walking with her legs wide apart, and stopping intermittently because of Braxton Hicks contractions. We haven't seen further evidence of the cougars, but we're all on edge. Predators will do that.

I'm thinking about that pistol. Where did it come from? It seems too new to have been Dad's. Did Leo bring it with him? That would mean he had it when the cougar attacked me. Why wouldn't he have used it then? The way it just showed up bothers me. The way he guards it.

I'm remembering something Griffin mentioned. He was checking out the old highway and spotted Leo from a distance coming down the mountain. Leo froze when he saw Griffin, then covered with a wave. He told Griffin he'd been hiking up to a lookout to survey Desolation Sound and see what other settlements were nearby and if they were inhabited. He never mentioned what he saw. I wonder if he has some kind of stash. I wonder if that's where the pistol came from. I wonder why.

I don't know what I just witnessed. I was on my way to the outhouse but decided I wanted a book to read and turned back. At the door to the house, something made me stop, hold the door open; it must have been a sound, I can't remember, but the hairs on the back of my neck stood up.

Don't. Parker's voice was strangely strangled.

That kid won't be able to keep this baby alive.

I should have waited to hear more but I walked in and let the door slam.

From the hall I heard a movement in the kitchen. I went to the kitchen. Leo was turning away from Parker who stood with her back to the counter, her hand covering her belly.

A simple no would have sufficed, he said for my benefit and walked out of the room. Parker started to cry. She waved me away.

I can see problems laid out for miles. Leo was always a law of the jungle type—his law, his jungle. He isn't giving up on getting Parker and he's obsessive when he zeroes in. I can only think of one plan. Two plans. I could suggest he go back with me to the city. I could say I needed to and that I can't do it alone. I'm almost certain he has no interest in leaving Nirvana though. He is staking a claim. Plan two is to keep things stable until Parker has her baby and then move her out of here. With Griffin if she wants and he wants, and the goats and the chickens. Leo can live happily ever after in Nirvana.

I can just see that.

I wonder if Parker will tell Griffin when he returns from fishing.

After dinner I went up to Leo's room. He was lying in bed, the covers under his armpits, reading some papers. He put them face down when I came in and never took his hand off them.

Whattup? he said with an ironic mimicry of ease.

I went in and sat in the chair in the corner, a low-slung thing with no arms that had been our great-grandmother's.

What was that this morning?

What was what?

Parker started crying when you left.

I guess I should take that as an insult.

How about a signal to leave her alone.

She's a big girl. She can take care of herself, believe me.

She's pregnant, Leo. And she's with Griffin.

She hasn't fully committed.

There were a bunch of framed photographs turned face down on the dresser near my chair. I turned one over. Our parents, arm in arm, in Palm Springs. A photo from another epoch. I got a stab of nostalgia.

Can I take this? He nodded. What are you up to, Leo? Up to?

Hey, I'm your brother. Something's going on.

But are you my keeper?

Yeah. Sure. Maybe I'll even keep you from yourself.

We were quiet for a bit.

The pistol. Parker. The cupboards. You're looking for something and you don't want to tell me about it.

I do things. The way everyone does, not *always* in a straight line.

But never without a purpose.

He shrugged. His feet moved under the covers. They distracted me for a moment, thinking about his bare feet. Why do I think you killed that goat?

We looked at each other. Why do you?

It wasn't lying right. A cougar would have eaten more. And dragged it into the bush. The cubs would have demolished it.

You're getting paranoid, big brother. Must be that post-stress thing. Why would I kill the goat? Although I admit I *was* getting sick of fish and shellfish and eggs.

The cougars didn't kill it. If they show up, I'm going to scare them off. I want the pistol to do it.

Yeah, well, let's see what Parker and Griffin think about that.

On this I don't care what they think.

Ooh, the boss rears his head. Leo put his hand behind his head, keeping the other on the papers.

What do you care? I asked. You don't even really want to live.

And now you do?

What are you reading?

Old love letters, he lied, not even bothering to disguise the lie, savouring his moment of dominance.

Bean and barley soup with a couple of goat bones, carrots and onion and thyme and sea salt. Good, but not quite enough to fill us. Leo held up a glass of goat's milk to Parker. Lovely soup, my dear. Thank you.

The last of the onions and the first of this year's carrots. I hope it's enough.

Oh God, Leo continued with a surge of emotion, when I think of how much food there was. And the variety. Sushi, wasabi, soy sauce! All gone. Your generation, he gestured with his spoon at Griffin, you don't know any different, but for me ... So many pleasures—and now—homespun, bland, and nourishing, for the rest of my life. Oh for a California Cab Sauv or a crisp French Chablis Grand Cru—and not just once, but every night ...

You're not helping, said Griffin.

Oh, *helping*. Everything going in one direction. Subsistence just isn't that engrossing for some of us older folk. Don't get me wrong. I love working out there in the field with you two, covering every millimetre of skin to avoid burnage, expending the same number of calories to do the work as to grow more calories, ad infinitum.

Leo's looking more like a mad man again these days. His hair is stiff with dirt and stands up at odd angles, and his beard looks like a squirrel has been tucking away food particles in there to last the winter. His eyes are a deeper blue than ever; the pupils always seem too small, and somehow he doesn't seem to see what he's looking at. We had to ask him to bathe and wash his clothes last week because he stinks. He tried to get us to wash them, saying it was our need not his.

I'm bored. I'm depressed. I want my old life back—my family, my car and my house, my clothes, restaurants, trips, movies. Variety! Variety! Variety! Variety! he shrieked, his eyes popping open, hand pounding on the table. Griffin and Parker remained very still.

It could be different, you know, he continued. It doesn't have to be like this. OneWorld Spartanism. They're hoarding. There's enough wealth. The one-child law has solved the problem; they're just not admitting it. They're fucking moralists without imagination. They've won, and they're imposing their morality on the world and loving the power. There are some who see what they're doing and are starting to organize. Getting ready. There are going to be changes. You should expect it.

He had my attention. What changes? I asked.

Leo looked at me, sizing me up, then an expression of contempt leaked over his face.

Oh change, change is inevitable, as the Buddha says.

I felt unbearably weary. More conflict. More striving. More history. More killing. I realized I had let myself believe that we were on the verge of a new order. A consensus after near extinction. Of course, there will be no end.

Leo spoke to Parker. At least you're having a baby. That's something new. Exciting. What is there for the rest of us?

What about your children? Parker asked, not looking at him.

Well, there's Griffin here, looking like the end of a line, and not, with all respect and affection to Griffin, even my bloodline. Allen over there has lost track of his boys, so that genetic covalent is a question mark, and I have lost my daughters. I'd hoped we'd find at least one of our offspring here, and that that one might know something about the others. Allen acts like it doesn't matter, but this could be the end of the Quincy line. All that's left is a few more stops at Barley Soup—no offense—and a blind date with the worms.

You can all be family to this baby, Parker said in a small burst of hopeful connectivity. It's not like it's going to have any other. It would be lucky to have three uncles. My mother used to say if a baby has good grandmothers or aunties, its chance for survival goes way up.

Charmed, I'm sure, to be compared to a grandma, and yes, of course, happy to be an uncle to the little thing. But, again, no offence—blood matters to me.

That was a conversation assassination and we stayed silent. Thicker than water, trickier than water. Leo put his bowl in the sink and left. Then Parker leaned in. What happened to his daughters?

I left home when I was sixteen, Griffin said. Amanda was nine and Annie was eight. I feel guilty now. I didn't know I was abandoning them. I didn't know Leo would leave. He stared at the woodstove. I was hoping to find some trace of them here.

I passed the staircase later that night on my way to bed and heard Parker and Griffin whispering furiously.

Leo came out of his room and stood at the top of the stairs with an empty jug in hand.

You know what they say, he winked as he went past to the kitchen to fill the jug with water. Loose hips sink ships.

This morning I got up early and made tea and porridge. Leo came down and we ate companionably enough. He tossed his spoon into the empty bowl, pushed back his chair, sucked air in through his teeth, and said, Gotta see a man about a logging operation.

He headed to the outhouse and I went up to his room and looked for the pistol. I looked under his pillow and his mattress, under the bed, in the drawers, in the wardrobe. I felt undignified skulking around and resented Leo for putting me in this position. I felt behind the books on the bookshelf. I checked the pockets of his clothes. I eliminated every possible place to hide a gun in that room. I thought about the papers he'd been reading and had lied to me about. There was a gap between the hardcover and the pages of one of the books in the bookcase, *For Whom the Bell Tolls*, by Ernest Hemingway. The papers were inside.

I took them out to the hallway where a narrow window looks onto the outhouse. Two copies of our parents' will. Everything looked standard, everything going to Leo and me fifty-fifty. The door to the outhouse slammed shut. There was a letter paper-clipped to the front of the second copy.

May 28, 2018
My Dear Sons,

I love you both so much. The times ahead are looking like they will be very tough and I want you both to know that your father and I have always hoped Nirvana could be a refuge for you and your families. You can always make do living here together, with the well and enough deer, waterfowl, shellfish, and firewood to last ten-thousand lifetimes. Your dad would be very happy at the thought.

Love
Mom

Leo clomped up the stairs. That stupid gun weighed down his coat pocket. I felt like smacking him just for taking the gun with him.

Why did you hide these from me?

You were in my room?

You were reading them last night.

I raised the hand with the papers. You should have shown them to me right away. We should have read them together. They're *our* parents.

There aren't any rules anymore. And stay the fuck out of my room.

I felt like strangling him. And where are Mom's ashes? I didn't see a container anywhere.

What do you think, I hucked them all over the place when the world was collapsing around me? A little backpack for Mom's remains, through thick and thin, carrying them with me, the good little son, through rain and shine, hurricane and drought, to sprinkle them on the ground here? I emptied them out at Fisherman's Terminal where the mini-ferries used to run. They floated out, like your fish food, and finally sank after half an hour. I can still smell the creosote.

I turned to leave, taking the will and the letter with me, the image of Mom's ashes in the filthy water shattering my heart.

Our parents. *Our* parents, he said bitterly to my back. You were right about one thing. Those papers don't make any difference.

I went into the old bathroom, which was the only room with a lock on the door, sat on the old flush toilet, and finished reading the will. It was all predictable except for the end. In the event of irreconcilable conflict between Leo and myself, the will stipulated that Nirvana, the land and the buildings, should go to me, while all remaining possessions should go to Leo. The reason given was that Leo's material resources far outweighed mine and therefore he had less need. I could just imagine how he'd loved reading that.

I missed Ruby intensely at that moment. I wanted to pack up and paddle back to the city. I wanted to be in her arms and hold her in mine and stare into her eyes and hear the throaty growl in her voice when she laughed. I stood up from the toilet and looked at myself in the mirror. The claw mark on my cheek, the patch of white folded skin and missing lip in the corner of my mouth, the raised pink scar near the hairline, the patchy hair—my face was a true testament to nurture over nature, though it looked more like nature than nurture. I don't recognize myself in it anymore.

I am deeply unsettled. I don't know what to do about Leo.

The next day Leo left early. He didn't tell me where he was going. All day the tension coming off Griffin was intense. Leo returned as we were sitting down for dinner.

So, *Dad*, Griffin spoke with a sarcasm lit by rage, were you ever going to tell me my sister was dead?

Leo looked at him through his hair. He took another bite.

I touched Griffin's arm. What?

Griffin stared at Leo, but addressed me. Parker knew my sister Anne from summer camp. She saw her in Victoria just before she came up here. Anne was looking for our mother, who disappeared a year after our sister died. Amanda died in Seattle in '42. Anne told Parker that that was the last time she saw her father. At the burial. Griffin enunciated each of the following words clearly: Piece of shit.

Leo continued to eat. Griffin reached across the table and grabbed Leo's forearm to stop the motion of fork to mouth. *I've lost my daughters? Blood matters?* Nothing matters to you.

You, Leo answered finally with contempt, don't know anything about me.

She was my sister! Griffin screamed at him. My sister! Griffin stood, pushing the table into Leo and me.

Leo looked at his fork, like he didn't know what to do with it, then threw it at the sink and stood.

She was my daughter! My daughter! You call me a piece of shit? You little fucker?

Griffin glared at Leo, but then sadness seemed to fill him and he left the room, followed by Parker. Leo got another fork and finished his food, then went to his room.

Today we worked on creating a primitive irrigation system for the field. There are only about three weeks during the summer when irrigation will be necessary, but they're important in the growing cycle. Some of our plants are turning brown. I feel weak and hot this morning and I have the beginnings of a mother of a headache. Leo and Griffin aren't speaking. Leo is monosyllabic with me.

Seeing Parker and Griffin together irritates me. They're discreet but it feels like they're making a show, even of their discretion. I almost understand why Leo keeps making a play. I yearn for Ruby and my alchemy with her. I don't want to die without making love with her again. I'm going to get this situation sorted and I'm going to paddle back after the baby is born and find her. I'll take Leo with me and we'll leave Griffin and Parker the harvest.

Griffin came to relieve me of shepherd duty and sat down beside me, saying that Leo had headed out with a daypack.

What makes Leo such a dick and you not?

Good question.

I mean, you come from the same family.

I looked across the field at the goats chewing grass. Actually, we didn't. I grew up in a family with parents who loved me. I'm not sure Leo did.

Because he was a dick.

I laughed and looked up at dark clouds scudding across the sky. Chicken and egg, I said.

An eagle turned, coming by for another look at the goats. What was Leo like? As a stepdad.

I was always glad he wasn't my real father. Griffin picked up a conifer cone and started to pull off the scales. He said all those stupid things like, "While I'm still paying for the roof over your head." I didn't give a shit, but Mom did. I guess he was paying for the roof over her head too. I used to provoke him. He was an easy target. Griffin made a neat pile of cone scales at his feet. I moved out to spare Mom more grief. He was making her choose between him and me.

We looked at the goats. The new kid, whose birth we celebrated a week ago just after the other one was killed, butted its mother's udder, then tugged hard on a teat.

Griffin took a big breath in, covered his eyes, and pinched his temples. I really hoped they'd be here, he said. This is the only place we all knew. He tossed the shredded cone into the field. Do you think he knows anything about my mother?

I thought about all of the deaths—they were like mushrooms in the forest. I didn't answer. Eventually I said, Amanda is lucky to be remembered by you.

Do you think Leo's dangerous? he asked.

Aren't we all, I thought. I answered, I don't know. I should get back though.

I entered the house through the basement door instead of the back porch where I usually come in. I heard a creak and a scuffle from above, as though someone were dragging a dog a short distance or they were losing their balance and regaining it with a quick movement of the feet. I closed the door carefully and listened. The floorboard creaked again.

I crept upstairs, bringing my fake foot down slowly, quietly. I emerged into the kitchen, smelled a soup cooking. I looked around the corner down into the hallway.

I could see my brother from the back, his pants at his ankles, one hand squeezing her breast, the other tugging her track pants down, and Parker's face turned sideways, eyes shut, arms protectively around her belly.

My brother heard me and turned, his erection sticking out sideways like an absurd thing, like Pinocchio's nose, the blue of his eyes dark with blood, a beast interrupted in the midst of a kill. He yanked his pants up, enraged by the indignity, and went up the stairs clutching them. Parker turned into the wall and pressed against it. I went up after my brother and threw open his door. He was doing up his belt. I lunged at him and threw him down, grabbed his hair, and smashed his head on the floor several times. He didn't resist. His eyes rolled in his head. I stopped. How do you think this can end? I screamed. His eyes gradually came back to focus, looking at me. There is no good way for this to end, I cried. We have to leave. We're leaving tomorrow.

He continued to lie on the floor and stare at the ceiling. Finally he said, I'm not leaving.

This morning I woke up with vertigo. Exhausted. Edged by memories of men taking the women aside at the border, the women shrinking in on themselves as they walked and the men inflating themselves, trying to give themselves the right. I was surrounded by a sense of doom.

Parker made cheese from the goat's milk yesterday and this evening she brought it out. She and Griffin made a small loaf of bread too.

The fat of the land, Leo said as he took a second piece. To think this is made of grass and water and a goat's digestive system. Parker, I'm impressed. As though he were lord of this fiefdom, and the food were an offering for him.

No one looked at him. Griffin showed only the usual contempt. Parker hasn't told him.

Eventually, ridiculously, I said, I haven't tasted anything this good for years either. Parker, how did you make it? Leo and I could start a business back in the canton. Start something new. Lay down a foundation. Look for our children. No time like the present. Leo, let's head back in the next couple of days. Griffin—sorry buddy, but I need to see Ruby. I think you can handle the baby's delivery. I know you can. And two less mouths to feed would be a bonus.

Leo stopped eating. He placed his hands on the table beside his plate. Took a big breath in.

Might as well cut my wrists right now. He looked at me. Remember before I came here? Really, give me a knife. He stood, picked up his plate, and took it upstairs with him.

We sat in silence for a while, Parker holding her belly. Why doesn't he just leave? Parker demanded. Griffin looked at her.

He found a will, I started.

He must have been listening at the top of the stairs. He came back down and threw his plate on the table.

This place is mine. You can ignore your birthright if you want, Allen, but I'm not going to. The rest of you can leave. My parents built this place. It's mine by blood.

If there's conflict between us, I started.

Conflict? he sneered. Is there *conflict* between us?

No one spoke. The crud of being human. A waste of goat cheese and bread.

When Griffin left with the goats today I made tea for Parker and myself. I wanted to talk to her. Leo had gone out before any of us got up.

If the three of us go to the city, I said, it's a six-day paddle. We find a place to live. Griffin and I can find work. We can keep the baby hidden.

She took a deep breath and looked at me. This baby is coming any day. She looked out the window. *He's* the one who should leave. Private property doesn't mean anything any more. There's no inheritance. There's no *blood*. She looked back at me. There's the three of us and there's him. He should leave.

He's not going to leave, I said.

You get the gun, point it at him, and tell him to leave. She blew on her tea. She had changed. She wasn't afraid anymore.

No matter how I tried to imagine that scene, the gun always went off. I looked away from her and stared out the window. My mind was racing, trying to stay ahead of the memories that were starting to whisper and gnaw at the edges of my mind, like nervous mice taking fast little bites. My hands started to shake. My eyes sank in their sockets.

He's my brother.

She looked directly at me. There's nothing as uncompromising as a woman thinking about the well-being of her child. Almost sociopathic. She comprehended all the implications of what she was saying and, for her, the final math was clear.

Say that worked, I said, trying to get my hands to stop trembling by pressing them hard against the table. You don't think he'd come back? You don't think he'd want revenge?

She sipped her tea. She didn't say any more.

We ate dinner in silence that evening. Leo finished first and put his plate in the sink. He turned to leave and Griffin said, Are you going to wash that?

Leo stopped, looking straight ahead.

Because *I'm* not. And there's no way Parker should. Uncle Allen—you?

I said nothing.

Leo picked his plate up as though to wash it, turned, and frisbeed it at Griffin's face. Griffin moved sideways.

The plate clipped his left temple, put a dent in the drywall behind him, and smashed onto the floor.

As good as washed, Leo said and stepped toward the door.

Griffin's chair hit the floor as he lunged across the room and tackled Leo. Leo fell against the counter, catching a bowl with his shoulder, which smashed on the floor just before he fell with Griffin on top of him. Griffin was not a fighter, but he was enraged. He got Leo by the throat and squeezed. Leo managed to grab a large piece of the broken bowl and slashed Griffin's forearm, then torqued his body and threw Griffin off. Leo sprang to his feet and launched a kick at Griffin's head, which snapped back. Parker screamed.

I roared something, got Leo in a headlock, and shoved him toward the door. He put his arms out and grabbed the doorjamb. Grinding the words out through clenched teeth he said, I've tried to get along with you people. I managed to dislodge one of his hands from the doorjamb and shoved him through. Fuck off Allen, he said, twisting out of my grip, I've had enough of this anyway. He went upstairs.

Griffin was confused and groggy, his arm bleeding heavily. Parker grabbed a clean towel and pressed it to stop the bleeding, while I tore up a pillowcase, butterflied the cut with tape, and bound it tight.

Parker leaned against the table suddenly, waiting out a contraction. I helped them up to their room and told Griffin to barricade the door and yell if he needed me. Before I left I said, We always used to fight over who did the dishes, but this one definitely takes the prize.

I woke up dreaming about Mom. She was kneading her hands like the agitator of a washing machine. She looked up at me with a blank expression. We never wanted *this*, she said.

This.

I'm freezing.

I can barely breathe. Everything feels old and dark, claustrophobic and old-school biblical. I yearn for something new, something fresh.

It's cloudy outside, but the clouds are high and white and there's a light breeze I wouldn't classify as wind. Sleep has left me exhausted. I feel like time has emptied its bucket on me. I don't feel any of the usual relief waking up, no *thank God it was only a dream.*

The sheets are damp from sweat. My head is pounding and my neck is stiff and I feel like I might puke.

I let the goats out of the shed. My turn for shepherd duty. I haven't told anyone how sick I'm feeling. I took a walking stick with me because I felt so weak and headed for the field past the old highway. Leo headed out first thing in the morning again with a daypack. Nonetheless I hate to leave Parker and Griffin.

I reached the old highway and needed a rest. I lay down in the middle of the road and looked up at the sky, listening to the off-key tinkling of the bells we made for the goats out of tin cans, wire, and stones. I was filled with wonder at the strange world I was in. White fluffy seeds floated everywhere, like warm snow, but even lighter, softer and airier. The goats stared at the fluff for a while, then put their heads back down to eat. A new kind of tree must have migrated north. I got up and continued to the field.

It was a sea of yellow weed flowers, opening in the light. I stood and gazed at the beauty until one of the goats lowered its head—and there she was, on the south edge, stone still except for her head turning slowly toward me. Even at that distance—thirty metres—the intentness of her gaze raised the hair on my arms. She didn't move. Nor did I.

All the problems at the cabin faded away. The sun broke through the clouds. She threw her head back, yawned, and vanished. The white seed pods twirled. In a hundred years some of them will be trees and she and I part of the earth that feeds them. *That's how she goes, and nobody knows, nobody knows, how cold my toes, my toes are growing.*

I felt dizzier then and vomited, begrudging the waste of food. I sat under a tree and leaned against its trunk. It also had white petals floating down to the earth, shaken free with each breeze. I must've dozed because the next thing I heard was Griffin's whistle. The sun was at its zenith behind the clouds.

I struggled to stand up, worried about the cougar—irrationally, because all the goats were fine. Griffin ambled up the hillside, nose still swollen, black eye turning yellow, looking happy.

These are amazing, he gestured up at the floating seeds.

Where's Parker? I asked anxiously. Another wave of dizziness hit me and I put my hand back to steady myself. A bulb of sap grabbed stickily at my palm.

Resting. Don't worry, she's barricaded in. He came back briefly but went out again. You were late. We were getting worried.

The cougar's here, I said. I saw her, only her, no cubs. Then I fell asleep. The goats are all here, right? Maybe she did kill that goat. Don't tell Leo. He's hunting her. He's obsessed with that thing.

Griffin gave me a quizzical look. You don't look good, Uncle Allen.

Griffin herded the goats back to the shed, and I went to bed. He came in to check on me, and I pulled him close and whispered, We need to get the pistol tonight. We have to act before I lose all my strength. I can't assume I'll get better.

I slept for the rest of the afternoon and into the night, feeling the cougar with me, following my thoughts. I was deep in a disaster dream trying to protect her when Griffin put his hand on my leg. I oriented myself, got dressed, slipped my knife in the holder, and we tiptoed upstairs. The wind was blowing hard enough to give us sound cover. I was shivering. I put my hand on Leo's doorknob.

I knew I was crossing a line, that if Leo woke it would be a fight brothers should never have, but he had already crossed so many lines. I didn't worry about being able to handle him, even being sick. He was a thrasher and I'd be in too close before he could get the pistol pointed let alone loaded.

I turned the knob and pushed.

The door opened a few centimetres and clunked into something. He'd pushed the dresser against the door. Clearly Leo didn't feel safe either. I felt like the hunter.

Wha'? Leo's voice called, half-asleep. Who's that?

I don't like lying.

I heard the cougar, I said. Out near the shed.

Shit. Hang on.

Leo moved the dresser. He was buttoning up his shirt. The pistol was shoved into the waist of his pants. I just took it and asked, Does it have a cartridge? Like we were in the same unit and we were going out to face the enemy.

In my pocket. He put his hand in his pocket to feel it.

In the kitchen I said, we should load it here, and held out my hand sideways, pretending to bend over and pick something up so we wouldn't be eye to eye.

Yeah, we should. Give me the gun and I'll do it.

I had the gun. I didn't need the cartridge.

Actually, Leo, I'm keeping it.

Leo looked from me to Griffin, who had moved close, hand on knife hilt. As he understood the betrayal, rage spread through him.

This is fucking war, he yelled and stormed back upstairs.

I put the pistol down my underwear. Griffin offered to take it, but I don't want Leo going after him. I collapsed back into bed.

You must kill him. If you don't, he'll kill you. Then we'll be here alone with him. Your brother is not a good man.

211

I woke, shivering and covered in sweat. The light hurts, I can't move my head. I dragged my covers into the living room where there's less light and collapsed on the couch. Our father watched from the end of the living room, then ducked back into the kitchen.

They brought me more blankets.

It was late afternoon and the sun was elongating the shadows of the tops of the conifers over the grass. Wild daisies, buttercups, clover, and dandelions were open in the heat. Ruby, naked, walked up to me and took my clothes off and spread them on the grass to make a blanket, then pulled me down beside her. She didn't speak a word. The bees were visiting the wildflowers around our head, as well as little orangey-brown moths, and above, blue and green dragonflies dipped and cleaned up mosquitoes.

She touched the wounds from the cougar attack and pressed her lips on them. I swooned with happiness and desire and joy. Nothing else mattered and everything else mattered. I heard the rush of wings over my head as a flock of small birds swooped and rollercoastered over the tree tops. A raven clicked from the edge of the clearing. Ruby's eyes were filled with light as she looked at me with a love unlike any I'd ever received. We were going to rollercoaster like those birds to wild and beautiful places.

I woke to silence. White seeds floating in the house. Someone must have left the door open. Something entered the kitchen.

I groped for the 9mm, but it wasn't there anymore. The cougar jumped up onto the kitchen counter. She was hungry now. If I called out for help she might attack. I stared at her.

When I next woke she was cradling my head in her paw, her rose-coloured tongue licking my face, her leg rubbing my thigh. She smiled—a Cheshire cat—teeth showing. I almost swooned with pleasure. The claw marks on my cheek sang and crackled. My mind shunted back, her tongue lifting traces of brain from my cheek and my sweat running like rain across bodies tinged blue, diluting their dried blood till it ran watery red to the ground.

Something fell clear in my mind, like a coin in a slot.

The seed pods floated down and covered everything with gossamer. I blinked, and the white down stuck to my eyelashes. The earth was covering herself with down.

I woke with this riddle in my mind. It had an aura of significance, like the feeling epileptics report just before a seizure.

> I open wide
> No teeth to hide
> My dear, they've long since crumbled!
>
> I take all comers
> Not fussy I
> But neither am I humbled
>
> With open thighs
> To girls and guys

I'm really quite a slut

Who resists
When I insist
A tryst upon my crust

A selfish mother
like no other
Your curfew's come around

Lay a wreath
And leave your teeth
Before you come to Mama

Who am I?

The cougar is gone. The seed pods are gone. The fever has
abated somewhat, but my head pounds. I hurt, I am weak.
Griffin came in with soup, his hands shaking. Leo's got the
pistol, he said.

I felt under me.

He saw the cougar. Out by the field. He's gone looking
for it.

No! I tried to stand.

I know, I know, Griffin said as though he understood.

He'll kill her for nothing, for living ... I started to pull
my pants on.

You're too sick, Uncle Allen. He won't get her, don't worry. Griffin made me get back into bed and spooned some soup into me.

He noticed the riddle and asked to read it. I am death? he guessed.

I am Mother Earth, I said.

Somehow I knew the answer.

The next time I opened my eyes the dirty knees of Leo's pants were in front of me. He was standing reading this journal.

I shut my eyes. I had to get it back before he read another word.

You can't kill the cougar, I said, keeping my eyes closed.

Who's going to stop me? Leo's voice was cold.

I'm asking you.

Who are you to ask me?

Your brother. Your brother's asking you.

The brother who tricked me?

Tricked you? How?

A chill went through me. The room closed in. What had I written down? *You must kill him. He's not a good man.* Had I written that down? Had he read it?

You know, Allen, your boys are better men than you. Better warriors.

How would you know? I pretended anger.

How would I know?

I'm asking.

I found them for you. But you didn't seem interested. Ruby had all your attention.

Where are they? I grabbed his arm. He closed the journal and held it in his other hand.

You sure you want to know?

Tell me.

I don't think I'm going to.

You lying fuck.

Temper, temper. And better watch your tongue. I'm pretty sure the new messiah doesn't swear.

Prove you saw them.

He opened my journal again and skimmed through the pages to the end.

I didn't know you were a poet too.

It's a riddle. Griffin figured out the answer, I lied.

He started to read it. For the first time since I woke I felt a small shift toward me. He wanted to guess the answer.

Griffin pounded down the stairs and ran in, eyes wide. I think her water broke.

Leo turned to him, his back to me. I directed Griffin wildly to the journal with my eyes. God bless him if he didn't walk right over and take the journal from Leo, lay it on the side table where I could reach it, and grab Leo's hand in both his.

Leo. Let's hit the reset button. We need to work together now.

Leo looked down at me. I wanted to grab the journal and slip it under the covers.

Griffin, I said, you remember everything I told you? Boiling water? Towels? Sterilize everything.

Leo extracted his hand from Griffin's. A moan came from upstairs. The look Leo gave me—I couldn't decode it—strangled, lonely, defiant. He left. Griffin ran back upstairs.

The thought of Leo reading the words *You must kill your brother* is making sirens go off in my head. Maybe he's thinking of murdering me now. Or Parker. Or all of us. Parker's panting is too fast upstairs. Griffin has come down, started the fire, and gone out to the well with the pails.

My heart pounds. The thought of Leo out there killing the cougar, just lifting the corner of that thought, makes me want to roar and bite and tear. He cannot be life's timekeeper. He cannot choose when she dies. He's a black hole, a lifesuck, a dead end, the end of the line—he does not have the right.

I got up and got my leg halfway into my pants, but the fabric was all twisted and in my frenzied rush my foot tore through, leaving the pant leg flapping like a flag behind my calf. I pulled on boots and grabbed my knife and walking stick. I must leave before Griffin returns and tries to make me stay.

I may not be able to finish my story after today. *I am thinking of murdering my brother*. A murder to ward off murder. I will murder murder with murder. What better man for the job?

I stopped and listened. My neck was frozen so I had to turn my whole body to hear. I turned a full circle. I felt like a giant. I heard the wind, nothing else. The light hurt my eyes. A longer louder moan from Parker rode out through the upstairs window. I started to hump and stump toward the field where he last saw her, the bottom half of my pant leg flapping in the wind. The wind was at my head, whipping my hair, trying to convince everything on the earth's surface—trees, grass, birds—to follow its lead. It pushed me toward the field.

The path was flanked by the root systems of ancient trees knocked over by storms. I passed a place where several trees had fallen against each other. The debris looked like the limbs of wrestling titans frozen in time, and something flashed across the base of my mind, a subliminal image made by me but unseeable, yet the dread tailing it was clear—the willy-nilly angles of branches and trunks against each other, the gouged earth, prone positions, circling back—*Finish the job, Mercy.*

A short distance ahead the bush was all blackberry, salal, young alder. A flash of red on my left made me look—a cluster of roses, spent but for the last few, a remnant of our mother's gardening, her tiny rebellion to plant it in the forest. I saw her in her plastic gardening clogs, baggy pants, and straw hat, squinting toward the future, squinting toward this moment.

A new wail from Parker shattered the vision and lit up my blood. The wail came on the wind pushing me forward, *if, if, if.* I burst onto the open field looking for the cougar, for

Leo. Nothing was there, yet the contour of the land meant I couldn't see the whole field at a glance—it was a hump of a field—to see the far side I'd have to make my way up toward the centre.

Great clods of earth lay where the hand plough had turned them over. I stumbled forward, the memory of Leo's hand on one side of the plough and mine on the other, three feet and a prosthesis pushing against the ground, driving the plough forward in case next year comes. My brother, Mr Big Time, the man who had to have servants or see himself a failure, bending himself to strain and sweat beside his brother.

I was fully exposed crossing the open field, yet it felt as though I was entering a boxed canyon. Wind blasted across the field and grabbed the trees on the edges and shook them, making their tops fly back and forth like the heads of children being shaken to death.

A quarter of the way across, on the far side, I spied the top of a head. It vanished. Reappeared. Vanished. It looked like a dried grey-brown cow pie. A few more steps and I saw the blade of a shovel rise to the sky and let fly a shower of dirt. What was he doing? Our work in the field was done. The seeds were planted and covered over. I looked down and saw the first tiny growths poking out from between clumps of dirt like albino worms timidly probing the open air, white from their subterranean, lightless births, with tiny heads of new green. I killed five or six with each step. Why was Leo tromping through our field, killing seedlings?

I paused. Whatever force I'd possessed to arrive here turned unstable and trembly, mired in the thick earth. I tried to lean on my walking stick, but its tip sank deep into the soft dirt. A clamouring chorus rose up from among the seedlings and I felt the hands of corpses just below the surface, waiting to grip my ankles and pull me down. I looked to the sky. I could only move forward, but the inertia gripping me was viscous and black as tar.

A crow flew over the field, turning its bright eye to look for food, flap, flap, flap, and I moved forward again over the clods of earth, like a man wearing cement shoes, gravity pulling me down.

Leo lifted the shovel to dig again but as he bent over, his head turned sideways in my direction. I stopped. He was wearing sunglasses. Would he greet me? Would he beckon me?

He stopped and stood up. Leaned on his shovel. He'd brought the wheelbarrow. I continued toward him.

If he looked at me with love, with quick affection, even just with welcome, I told myself I wouldn't kill him. A deal with God, with fate, *do this one thing*. A wager made in a mirror, dealer's eyes meeting player's—twins winking.

I got within six or seven metres. Leo smiled, but he showed lots of teeth. It couldn't be described as friendly.

I advanced, thinking, Leo's feet must be as heavy as mine. But when I approached, I noticed that his pants were folded up and he was barefoot. He was going to be lighter and faster, though he'd have less traction. I stopped. Leo's smile thinned to a sneer or a taunt, though not necessarily malicious, and he cocked his head slightly. *Oh ho, so that's how it is*, his smirk could be saying, or *For all your fine talk*. It could also have meant, *What do you want?*

Speak, Leo, say my name. Let me hear warmth in your throat.

He bent back down to his work and drove the blade of the shovel into the ground, leaving me standing there, awkward, lumbering, off balance. The sound of stone and grit against metal made the enamel of my teeth hurt. Because of the high furrows and my position on the hill, I could not see what kind of hole he was digging.

I clumped forward a few more steps. My peripheral vision was snagged by something on the left, an unexpected brightness in the landscape. I looked away from Leo to see what it was. A chequered tablecloth floated just above the earth, held up, I guessed, by the stubble of the dried, cut wild grass.

A picnic? Here? Now?

Leo stood straight again, removed his sunglasses, and wiped the sweat from his brow. I saw a mark across his temple into his greying hair, a smear of red. Was it there before he wiped the sweat from his face?

The time for questions was now. If I failed to ask what he was doing it would either seem as though I already knew or didn't care. The crow flew over again, this time followed by a gang of crows. A murder of men. Their flyby focused over Leo and where he was digging.

The shape of a body took form in my mind—bloody, heavy, lifeless, the tablecloth a shroud—the scrape of shovel blade against stones the sound of a grave being dug.

This was the moment. Were the figments of my mind bound to what was real, or were they nightmare visions thrown up by a psyche that had raced between horror and the mundane for far too long? Was it possible he would leave? Would he play nice? I faced my brother, wanting to ask what he was doing, but asking was a submissive act; it left you waiting for an answer, vulnerable to a lie. And as I stood I knew there was no point in asking because I could neither believe nor disbelieve his answer. I had to proceed without cover of words and see what my eyes saw.

What are you doing? I asked.

Leo looked down at his feet.

Trickery is so much better than murder, but trick tock, trick tock, I couldn't think of any tricks. Minutes went by and the silence started to say too much. The more time passed, the more precise became the silence's meaning. No need for the junk of speech.

What did the silence say to Leo? It was this uncertainty, this territory that I couldn't quite see that allowed me to hesitate, that trapped me in a pause. I was the player in his play. I had to wait. Something would be revealed. No amount of patience would prevent that.

Leo looked me in the eye. I got her at the chickens, he said. He turned to indicate the body and I saw her in my mind's eye, stretched out, a sacrifice on the altar, because he had no reason to live and could not die. Destruction spread out from him like blood from a cut jugular, and I felt the silent click of a switch turning on. I raised my walking stick in both hands, took it back, and swung it at the back of his head. His head snapped forward then bobbled back, but the tension leaked out of his body. He fell to his knees. I stepped back in preparation to strike him again, though by then I'd rather have killed myself. I struck two more times and heard the sound, like a thick eggshell, not on the edge of a glass but dropped on a floor.

I flung the stick away from me.

In the furrow behind the tablecloth, the long body of the cougar nestled in the milky-brown earth, her small flat head partly severed from her body. I stroked her head between the ears. Her body wasn't cold yet. I touched the blood on her chest then licked my finger so that she could also travel in me as I had in her.

The pistol lay unused beside the tablecloth. I checked. The cartridge was full. Nothing had been revealed.

I screamed at the sky, at whatever had created me, at whatever had created this, because nothing seemed like Leo's fault anymore. I screamed and screamed until my voice broke and I had no more strength.

I knelt down and lifted my brother's broken head in my lap. I stroked his forehead and kissed him and wept and told him how sorry I was.

Then I went back to the cabin. I walked upstairs. Griffin was holding the baby. Parker was pale and sweaty, but blissful. I was covered in dirt and my brother's blood.

This must be the last, I yelled. My eyes burned into her. Do you hear me? What I have done for you must be the last. It is on you to start something new.

A sob strangled my voice. I howled and the baby cried, but I didn't care. That baby must know what it owed its life to. Griffin handed the howling baby to Parker and came toward me.

I looked at Parker and she met my gaze. She was all mother at that moment, which meant feral and ruthless. She couldn't feel anything that wasn't related to her baby. I willed her to tell him.

Leo assaulted Parker, I said. She flinched. And then he refused to leave.

Griffin turned to Parker.

I didn't want the baby to get hurt.

I left. I could feel their belief in their goodness, in their good intentions, in each other's good intentions, and that belief was too big a gulf. They believed they were separate from Leo, that they were made of different stuff from him. They'd never understand. They hadn't been in the furrow, holding his head. They hadn't heard his skull break. They hadn't loved him. I belonged with him now.

I went down to the kitchen to clean my hands. I needed to be clean to think. A bowl of apples sat on the table, yellow ones, transparent, first of the season. Hours ago, those apples would have been for me, but they were no longer. I was in a state of Nirvana, conscious but free of desire. I was a piece of wood. I drank water, knowing the rivers owed me nothing, and drank anyway, because what I did didn't matter anymore.

When Leo fell I glimpsed his profile, and what it telegraphed was so uncomplicated, so unjudging. So, it's you after all, he might have said. It's you who are the murderer. Not me. Or, You didn't love me and I thought you did. Or, Oh well, it doesn't matter. When he fell, one eye looked at dirt and the other at my ankle.

Upstairs there were murmurs and a kittenish cry. I decided to go back out to the field and join my brother in his feast of dirt. I wished I'd told him I'd be keeping him company.

The crows waited for me on the humps of the furrows, loosely gathered like a sidewalk audience after a talented busker starts packing up. They scattered reluctantly but alighted again a short distance away. Leo hadn't left, which surprised me, weirdly. I looked up at the sky, the grey sky, that upside-down cup of a firmament, and it looked unhinged and unfirm, and I found it strange that I could not see past the light into the ocean of blackness beyond, found it strange that I was stuck in night's opposite when I was so close to returning to those dark and soundless skirts.

I would go to ground between my companions. I'd put my arm around my brother's shoulders and lay my head on the cat's soft belly, raise the pistol to my head, and pull the trigger. I imagined the crows startling and flapping up, circling in alarm, ready to depart at a second shot but, hearing none, re-alighting amidst the stubble and being there to greet Griffin when he came to see what happened.

The hole Leo had been digging was neither deep nor wide enough for the three of us, so I started to dig. When it was about three feet deep, I lowered myself in and grabbed one fore paw and one hind paw and pulled the cougar toward me. She thumped into the hole on her back. I heaved her onto her side, then climbed out and went for Leo. I lifted his feet, hooked one under each arm and drove forward, pitting my weight against his. I moved him inch by inch. At the graveside I pulled him around so his head would land beside her head and climbed back in. I pulled first his arm, then his leg, alternating until he thumped in beside her. I shoved him closer to her until he lay inside her embrace. Then I placed her forepaw on his upper arm and placed his arm across her belly. Her head rested near his chest just below his chin. I looked down, heart pounding from exertion, and realized I'd left no room for myself in the middle. And that decided it. The worms would have to wait. The grey sky swirled around me. I climbed out and filled the grave.

I threw my things into a dry bag and went to the kitchen to pack some food. Griffin came down. I told him where to lay a stone if he wanted. He cried and asked if I'd be returning. I held his face and kissed his forehead, then gave him the pistol and the cartridge. I told him I thought Leo might have had a weapons cache in the area. It was even possible, I said, that Leo had connections to the resistance and that they might come looking for the weapons. I counselled him to find the cache and get rid of the weapons.

He came with me down to the water. A low-lying fog had oozed down from the hills, and there was a chill in the air. I loaded the hatch, slid the kayak into the water, and climbed in. I paddled out a few strokes, turned the boat around, and yelled back to the shore, Never again! and began to laugh. Never again! I yelled as I turned back out toward the strait and yelled it over and over, laughing maniacally until tears streamed down my cheeks. I paddled away. Eventually the fog absorbed my words. The cold brine of the Georgia Strait trickled down onto my hands.

Now, on this beach, decamped a day's paddle away, I've written my story until this moment.

I am having visions. I know they're visions. Grandiose visions that I committed some kind of last murder. I understand that my mind is throwing up these visions to make my torment bearable. My mind wants me to survive though my body is not well.

I've built a small sweat lodge using a tarp and branches dug into the sand. Every day I build a fire, heat the rocks, transfer them inside, and pour river water over them. If I am to return I must get clean. As clean as possible.

While looking for the right rocks to heat, I found a rock with a smooth surface like a tablet. Every day I chisel a few words on it. They are different than what I write here in the journal. They have a different weight. When I'm finished carving I believe I'll be ready to travel again.

This morning a cougar walked past me on the beach. I was staring out to sea after a sweat and it walked right past, by the water's edge. A young male. He looked at me. It was her son, I thought.

I have finished what I was chiselling. I transcribe the words here:

> And Allen slew Leo in a field. The earth drank the blood of the one and the tears of the other. I am a man of peace but look at the work of my hands. This is the last murder. A new covenant begins. From this day forward people shall know the murder of one is the murder of all and there is no future in it. I will turn a blind eye no more and I shall weep. My mark is on Allen that everyone may know he is a man and be wary. He will remain among his people until his dying days, a peaceful man of the hearth. Nonetheless whoever harms him will be forgiven sevenfold.

Amid the gentle din of people heading home from work, I lean against a wall and stare up at clouds lightening and darkening, depending on their fullness. A thrumming sounds in my ear. I turn to see the cause and catch a blur in the direction of a late-blooming rosebush near the building's entrance. Above one of the blooms a green hummingbird hovers, a slash of red at its throat. It plunges its beak into the flower's centre.

Then I hear the sound, the familiar cadence, the brisk stride, *clack, clack, clack*. I open my bag and take out a red sandal, which I place upright in the palm of my shaking hand. I stretch my arm out, waiting. Why not? None of us deserves to be here.

I am marked, but I have survived.

Log of Deaths: Canton Number Three, Cascadia, October 27, 2054

Allen Levy Quincy, of a heart attack, age 64. Predeceased by wife Jennifer (née Arcand) in 2030. Mourned by companion Ruby Blades, nephew Griffin (Parker), and great-niece, Anne. The whereabouts of two sons, Luke and Sam, are unknown. Also whereabouts of a brother, Leo Dermid Quincy, is unknown.

Updated, May 8, 2073
Also mourned by son Sam Quincy (Maud), granddaughter Marie (Eric), and great-grandson Smoke. The whereabouts of son Luke Quincy is still unknown. The human remains found on Forgotten Peninsula, Vancouver Island are presumed to be those of Leo Dermid Quincy

ACKNOWLEDGEMENTS|

Thanks to Michael Baser—everyone should have such a champion—and my fairy god-sister Jamie Lee Curtis. Thanks to my agent Phyllis Wender, whose painstaking perseverance helped make this book what it is, and to her assistant Allison Cohen for work behind the scenes. Thanks to Chris Hennebery for information and proofreading about military structure and weapons, and war photographer Gary Knight for a discussion about killing. Thanks to Thad McIlroy for helping me keep the faith, and Shefa Siegel, who inspired the scene of berries. Thanks to Aislinn Hunter and John Colapinto, comrades in the trenches. Thanks to Anne Giardini for early support, and for excavating the title. Thanks to Sarah Chase, whose generosity in talking about her art as a choreographer provided invaluable research. Thanks to many readers whose literary biofeedback was essential: Betsy Warland, Nancy Richler, Anne Collins, Bill Marchant, Ian MacPherson, Maureen Palmer, Helen Slinger, Nadine Schuurman, Myriam Casper, Sarah Maitland, and Gavin Hollett.

Thanks to everyone at Arsenal Pulp Press—Brian, Susan, Cynara, and Oliver. Making this book with you was "simply the best," to quote Tina Turner.

I want to acknowledge Hornby Island, British Columbia, whose ample beauty and brilliantly resourceful inhabitants continue to expand me.

Thanks to Samantha Power, Romeo Dallaire, and Gwynne Dyer for their writing about genocide, post-traumatic stress disorder, and climate change, and to all the people marching in the streets, all the people working to turn this ship around.